The Winning Tickets

A Standalone Novel

Judith Keim

Praise For Judith Keim's Novels

THE BEACH HOUSE HOTEL SERIES – Books 1-6:

"Love the characters in this series. This series was my first introduction to Judith Keim. She is now one of my favorites. Looking forward to reading more of her books."

BREAKFAST AT THE BEACH HOUSE HOTEL is an easy, delightful read that offers romance, family relationships, and strong women learning to be stronger. Real life situations filter through the pages. Enjoy!"

LUNCH AT THE BEACH HOUSE HOTEL – *"This series is such a joy to read. You feel you are actually living with them. Can't wait to read the latest one."*

DINNER AT THE BEACH HOUSE HOTEL – "A Terrific Read! As usual, Judith Keim did it again. Enjoyed immensely. Continue writing such pleasantly reading books for all of us readers."

CHRISTMAS AT THE BEACH HOUSE HOTEL – "Not Just Another Christmas Novel. This is book number four in the series and my introduction to Judith

Keim's writing. I wasn't disappointed. The characters are dimensional and engaging. The plot is well crafted and advances at a pleasing pace. The Florida location is interesting and warming. It was a delight to read a romance novel with mature female protagonists. Ann and Rhoda have life experiences that enrich the story. It's a clever book about friends and extended family. Buy copies for your book group pals and enjoy this seasonal read."

MARGARITAS AT THE BEACH HOUSE HOTEL – "What a wonderful series. I absolutely loved this book and can't wait for the next book to come out. There was even suspense in it. Thanks Judith for the great stories."

"Overall, Margaritas at the Beach House Hotel is another wonderful addition to the series. Judith Keim takes the reader on a journey told through the voices of these amazing characters we have all come to love through the years! I truly cannot stress enough how good this book is, and I hope you enjoy it as much as I have!"

THE HARTWELL WOMEN SERIES – Books 1 – 4:

"This was an EXCELLENT series. When I discovered Judith Keim, I read all of her books back to back. I thoroughly enjoyed the women Keim has written about. They are believable and you want to just jump into their lives and be their friends! I can't wait for any upcoming books!"

"I fell into Judith Keim's Hartwell Women series and have read & enjoyed all of her books in every series. Each centers around a strong & interesting woman character and their family interaction. Good reads that leave you wanting more."

THE FAT FRIDAYS GROUP – Books 1 – 3:

"Excellent story line for each character, and an insightful representation of situations which deal with some of the contemporary issues women are faced with today."

"I love this author's books. Her characters and their lives are realistic. The power of women's friendships is a common and beautiful theme that is threaded throughout this story."

THE SALTY KEY INN SERIES – Books 1 – 4:

FINDING ME – "I thoroughly enjoyed the first book in this series and cannot wait for the others! The characters are endearing with the same struggles we all encounter. The setting makes me feel like I am a guest at The Salty Key Inn...relaxed, happy & light-hearted! The men are yummy and the women strong. You can't get better than that! Happy Reading!"

FINDING MY WAY - "Loved the family dynamics as well as uncertain emotions of dating and falling in love. Appreciated the morals and strength of parenting throughout. Just couldn't put this book down."

FINDING LOVE – "I waited for this book because the first two was such good reads. This one didn't disappoint.... Judith Keim always puts substance into her books. This book was no different, I learned about PTSD, accepting oneself, there is always going to be problems but stick it out and make it work. Just the way life is. In some ways a lot like my life. Judith is right, it needs another book and I will definitely be reading it. Hope you choose to read this series, you will get so much out of it."

FINDING FAMILY – "Completing this series is like eating the last chip. Love Judith's writing, and her female characters are always smart, strong, vulnerable to life and love experiences."

"This was a refreshing book. Bringing the heart and soul of the family to us."

THE CHANDLER HILL INN SERIES – Books 1 – 3:

GOING HOME – "I absolutely could not put this book down. Started at night and read late into the middle of the night. As a child of the '60s, the Vietnam war was front and center so this resonated with me. All the characters in the book were so well developed that the reader felt like they were friends of the family."

"I was completely immersed in this book, with the beautiful descriptive writing, and the authors' way of bringing her characters to life. I felt like I was right inside her story."

COMING HOME – "Coming Home is a winner. The characters are well-developed, nuanced and likable. Enjoyed the vineyard setting, learning about wine growing and seeing the challenges Cami faces in running and growing a business. I look forward to the next book in this series!"

"Coming Home was such a wonderful story. The author has such a gift for getting the reader right to the heart of things."

HOME AT LAST – "In this wonderful conclusion,

to a heartfelt and emotional trilogy set in Oregon's stunning wine country, Judith Keim has tied up the Chandler Hill series with the perfect bow."

"Overall, this is truly a wonderful addition to the Chandler Hill Inn series. Judith Keim definitely knows how to perfectly weave together a beautiful and heartfelt story."

"The storyline has some beautiful scenes along with family drama. Judith Keim has created characters with interactions that are believable and some of the subjects the story deals with are poignant."

SEASHELL COTTAGE BOOKS:

A CHRISTMAS STAR – "Love, laughter, sadness, great food, and hope for the future, all in one book. It doesn't get any better than this stunning read."

"A Christmas Star is a heartwarming Christmas story featuring endearing characters. So many Christmas books are set in snowbound places...it was a nice change to read a Christmas story that takes place on a warm sandy beach!" Susan Peterson

CHANGE OF HEART – "CHANGE OF HEART is the summer read we've all been waiting for. Judith Keim is a master at creating fascinating characters that are simply irresistible. Her stories leave you with a big smile on your face and a heart bursting with love."

~Kellie Coates Gilbert, author of the popular Sun Valley Series

A SUMMER OF SURPRISES – "The story is filled with a roller coaster of emotions and self-discovery. Finding love again and rebuilding family relationships."

"Ms. Keim uses this book as an amazing platform to

show that with hard emotional work, belief in yourself and love, the scars of abuse can be conquered. It in no way preaches, it's a lovely story with a happy ending."

"The character development was excellent. I felt I knew these people my whole life. The story development was very well thought out I was drawn [in] from the beginning."

A ROAD TRIP TO REMEMBER – "I LOVED this book! Love the character development, the fun, the challenges and the ending. My favorite books are about strong, competent women finding their own path to success and happiness and this is a winner. It's one of those books you just can't put down."

"The characters are so real that they jump off the page. Such a fun, HAPPY book at the perfect time. It will lift your spirits and even remind you of your own grandmother. Spirited and hopeful Aggie gets a second chance at love and she takes the steering wheel and drives straight for it."

THE DESERT SAGE INN SERIES – Books 1 – 4:

THE DESERT FLOWERS – ROSE – "The Desert Flowers - Rose, is the first book in the new series by Judith Keim. I always look forward to new books by Judith Keim, and this one is definitely a wonderful way to begin The Desert Sage Inn Series!"

"In this first of a series, we see each woman come into her own and view new beginnings even as they must take this tearful journey as they slowly lose a dear friend. This is a very well written book with well-developed and likable main characters. It was interesting and enlightening as the first portion of this saga unfolded. I very much enjoyed this book and I do recommend it"

"Judith Keim is one of those authors that you can always depend on to give you a great story with fantastic characters. I'm excited to know that she is writing a new series and after reading book 1 in the series, I can't wait to read the rest of the books."!

THE DESERT FLOWERS – LILY – "The second book in the Desert Flowers series is just as wonderful as the first. Judith Keim is a brilliant storyteller. Her characters are truly lovely and people that you want to be friends with as soon as you start reading. Judith Keim is not afraid to weave real life conflict and loss into her stories. I loved reading Lily's story and can't wait for Willow's!"

"The Desert Flowers Lily is the second book in The Desert Sage Inn Series by author Judith Keim. When I read the first book in the series, The Desert Flowers-Rose, I knew this series would exceed all of my expectations and then some. Judith Keim is an amazing author, and this series is a testament to her writing skills and her ability to completely draw a reader into the world of her characters."

THE DESERT FLOWERS – WILLOW – "The feelings of love, joy, happiness, friendship, family and the pain of loss are deeply felt by Willow Sanchez and her two cohorts Rose and Lily. The Desert Flowers met because of their deep feelings for Alec Thurston, a man who touched their lives in different ways."

"Once again, Judith Keim has written the story of a strong, competent, confident and independent woman. Willow, like Rose and Lily can handle tough situations.

All the characters are written so that the reader gets to know them but not all the characters will give the reader warm and fuzzy feelings."

"The story is well written and from the start you will be pulled in. There is enough backstory that a reader can start here but I assure you, you'll want to learn more. There is an ocean of emotions that will make you smile, cringe, tear up or outright cry. I loved this book as I loved books one and two. I am thrilled that the Desert Flowers story will continue. I highly recommend this book to anyone who enjoys books with strong women."

The Winning Tickets

A Standalone Novel
Sail Away Series
Book Seven
Judith Keim
Wild Quail Publishing

Copyright

ISBN# 978-1-959529-48-4

Cover by Elizabeth Mackey Graphic Design

Dedication

For Peter, who shares his love of sailing with me.

Books By Judith Keim

Christmas Stories – Soul Sisters Anthology

Christmas Joy – (2022)

THE SANDERLING COVE INN SERIES:

Waves of Hope

Sandy Wishes – (2023)

Salty Kisses – (2023)

THE LILAC LAKE INN SERIES

Love by Design – (2023)

Love Between the Lines – (2023)

Love Under the Stars – (2024)

OTHER BOOKS:

The ABC's of Living With a Dachshund

Once Upon a Friendship – Anthology

Winning BIG – a little love story for all ages

Holiday Hopes

The Winning Tickets – (2023)

For more information: www.judithkeim.com

The Winning Tickets

By Judith Keim

Prologue

G abby Willetts straightened her navy blazer, pushed back a lock of chestnut-brown hair from her face, and took a deep breath. She could do this. She'd held her own all month and now had just two days to go before the Caribbean Cruise contest was over. After the difficult year she'd had, she needed to win, wanted to get away and have a little fun.

She walked across the sales floor to greet the new arrivals. She liked working as a salesperson at Dan Davis Motors, a Lexus dealer in Ellenton, a town in upstate New York. Some thought it odd that she'd chosen to work at a car dealership, but after being raised by a single dad who loved tinkering with cars for both a job and a hobby, she knew a lot more about cars than people might guess from her stylish appearance. The fact that she'd been an assistant to a successful financial consultant in New York City meant she knew the ins and outs of corporate and retail finance too.

Out of the corner of her eye, she noticed Hank Davis rising from his desk and heading to the door to greet the couple who'd just walked into the showroom. He was a tall man with classic features, butterscotch hair, and light-blue eyes and was very good at his job. They'd competed from the beginning. Being the owner's son gave him a slight edge, but she'd kept up with him.

She smiled at the man and woman standing by the entrance. "Hello, I'm Gabby Willetts. May I help you? I'd love to show you around and tell you about some of the deals we can offer."

"Thanks. That would be great," said the woman smiling at her. "The car is for me."

Her husband noticed Hank and turned to him. "Maybe you can help us."

Hank shook his hand. "Welcome to Dan Davis Motors. Ready to talk cars? With our help, you'll be able to drive one of these cars off the lot today."

Though she was burning inside at the way Hank was about to take over, Gabby took the arm of the woman. "Why don't we take a look around?"

"That would be nice," the woman replied. "I know what I want, but I don't like shopping for cars. I find it confusing." She held out her hand. "I'm Robin Woods, and that's my husband, Bill, over there."

Gabby shook her hand. "Pleased to meet you. Let's have some fun, shall we?" As they walked around, Gabby chatted with Robin and quickly discovered she was a quilter, had one grandson and another on the way, spoiled a Yorkshire Terrier, and lived in a house on the outskirts of their town. With this information available, Gabby showed her a couple of sedans then discussed three different-size SUVs.

They talked about comfort and ease and driving features in all of them, taking a moment to get themselves bottles of water as they continued discussing options about cars and life in general.

Gabby and Robin approached Hank and Bill sometime later as the men were standing by a sports coupe looking under the hood.

Robin grinned at her husband. "Hey, Bill, I've decided on the car I want. Even the color. Gabby has been wonderful to work with."

Bill's mouth opened with astonishment. "That's awfully quick. Are you sure? Hold on; I've been talking with Hank here."

"Yes, and while you've been doing that, Gabby and I have arrived at a decision," said Robin smoothly. "*We're* doing the purchase through Gabby," she continued with surprising strength. "You and I talked about buying a Lexus before we came here, and I'm more than satisfied with what Gabby and I discussed."

Gabby turned to Bill. "We can go into my office to discuss prices and do the paperwork. I'm certain we can arrive at an agreement that will please you."

Dan, Hank's father and the dealership owner, walked over to them with a look of concern. "Is there a problem here?"

"Absolutely not," said Robin, moving closer to Gabby. "I love the service Gabby has given me. She answered all of my questions, and we worked through the best choice for me. You're very lucky to have someone on staff who makes it so easy."

Dan smiled, making his blue eyes shine. "You're not the first one to tell me that. Gabby knows our products and understands what's under the hood as much as anyone else here." He turned to her. "Keep this up, Gabby, and you'll win that ten-day Caribbean cruise."

"A cruise? How delightful!" Robin said to her. "I have a friend who's looking for a new car. I'll send her in and tell her to ask for you."

"Thanks," said Gabby. "If I win, I'm planning on surprising my best friend with the cruise. A girls' getaway."

Robin took hold of Gabby's arm and beamed at her. "I'll be rooting for you."

Gabby didn't dare look at Hank. They were neck and neck in the race for the prize. She had only a couple of days to surge ahead of him by selling more cars than he.

"Okay, I guess that's it," said Bill. "Once Robin makes up her mind, I have no choice. Nice talking to you, Hank. Gabby, show me the way to your office, and we'll get this settled."

Bill was a tough negotiator, but Gabby had no problem getting approval on the deal from Dan, probably because of the hope of referrals from Robin.

After Bill and Robin left with the understanding that they'd pick up their car the next day, newly washed and gassed up, Gabby was exhausted but happy. She sat at her desk putting the paperwork together for Dan and the financial manager.

Hank popped his head into the office. "That may be another deal for you, but I'm pretty sure I'm closing one this afternoon. Then, watch out! The woman I've started seeing thinks I'm winning the cruise for her."

Gabby grinned. "I've worked hard for this, and I'm not giving up a chance for a cruise like this. It's March winter weather here, and I'm dying to get away to sun, sand, surf and all the fun." She didn't say it, but she thought his new girlfriend, Ashley, was a spoiled brat who'd probably find fault with the cruise and wouldn't even go near one of the ship's buffets. What a waste.

"Ashley told me that you and she were never friends in high school," said Hank. "What's that all about?"

Gabby worked hard to keep a pleasant look on her face. "No, we weren't friends." Ashley had been one of four girls who'd made high school miserable for Gabby because she didn't have the money to buy the expensive designer clothes they liked. What she did have was a friend, the boy next door, whom they all wanted to date. Dwayne wasn't interested, and only Gabby knew why. Today, Dwayne and his husband were happy living on the west coast. She'd always be grateful to him for his kindness to her. She would never have made it through high school without Dwayne's friendship, her father's support, and Jessica Knight, her BFF since grade school.

Her father had been a wonderful dad, showering her with love and attention even through the tough years when she was a teenager ridden with angst about her figure and the fact that she couldn't seem to fit in. "Gabby, sweetheart, you're beautiful inside and out," he'd told her over and over again. It was a soothing phrase she hadn't believed until she lived and worked in New York City away from her detractors. She'd recently returned to Ellenton to live when her father became ill with cancer. Now, at thirty-two, and after his passing, she was content to stay in town to enjoy a simpler life.

Gabby and Hank both turned as a voice trilled, "Hank! There you are. What are you doing in Gabby's office?"

Hank whipped around. "Talking business. Why are you here?"

Ashley breezed into the office, threw her arms around Hank, and gazed up at him with a pleading look and pouty smile. She was a thin, striking woman with blond hair and green eyes that flared when she didn't get her way. "Thought you might like to take me out to dinner this evening. I bought a new outfit for the occasion."

"Excuse me," said Gabby. "I need to deliver these papers." She eased out of her office past the hugging couple. No way did she want to be part of that scene. Ashley deceived many people with her cute little games, but Gabby knew the true person beneath the beautiful exterior.

When she went to his office to deliver the papers to Dan, he waved her to a chair. "Sit down, Gabby. I want to compliment you again for taking care of customers and making them feel right at home here. I know you're competing against Hank for the cruise, but no matter what, I appreciate all you do here. It's especially nice because I know your father would be proud. For years, he was our best auto mechanic and a real friend of mine."

"Thanks," said Gabby. "I was thinking of my father earlier."

"A good man, Bob Willetts," said Dan. "Good luck with the contest."

She grinned and rose. "Thanks."

That night, Gabby let herself into the condo she'd purchased after selling the house she and her father had lived in. She'd been happy to make the break from the past by moving away from it. She'd always remember and be grateful for the talks she and her father had as he lay ill. They'd agreed that the point of living was to try to enjoy each day, treat others with respect, and give what you could of time and resources to help them.

Gabby had taken those words to heart. Though she wasn't ready for children of her own, she'd agreed to become a "big sister" to a little girl in foster care who needed extra attention. At three, Saree was an adorable handful who'd been born with Fetal Alcohol Spectrum Disorder. She was behind in development, but she responded to certain stimuli with a sweet smile that kept her family and Gabby working toward new growth. Gabby spent some afternoons when she wasn't working and occasional evenings watching Saree to give her foster parents a break. They had two boys of their own and were thrilled by her participation.

Tonight, after changing her clothes, Gabby was going to help them. Since she'd come back to town, she hadn't really dated. She'd gone out a couple of times with one of the mechanics at the dealership with the understanding they were just friends. When the time came for something more, Gabby wanted it to be with the right man with all the tingly sensations she'd read about in novels. In the City, she'd had plenty of dates, but they hadn't gotten serious because she was still waiting for those tingles.

The next morning, Gabby woke up with a resolution to make a sale. One more might do it. Hank had made his sale, catching up to her.

Excited by the idea of beating him at this game, she got out of bed and prepared for the day. Each sale brought her satisfaction, but having the cruise as a prize made it even better.

Later that morning, two couples came into the dealership at the same time. Hank took one; she took the other.

When she realized the young couple was just looking, Gabby's heart sank. She glanced at Hank, talking with excitement as he led his people over to one of the sportier models.

"Let me gather brochures for you," Gabby said sweetly to the young couple, respecting their decision. "Take your time, look them over, and after you study them, I'd be happy to talk to you about any opportunities we can make to give you the right choice. Call me anytime."

"Thanks. It's a big investment for us," said the cute young woman who was obviously pregnant.

"Yes, buying a car always is. But the safety this vehicle provides is important for any growing family. My father worked here for years, and I know the high quality of these cars," Gabby said with a note of pride. "The safety ratings are outstanding."

Seeing their interest, Gabby led them over to an SUV.

After going over everything, the couple thanked Gabby and said they might be in touch later.

Disappointed, Gabby waved them off, noting that Hank was still talking to the couple with him.

Gabby went into her office and told herself to relax. She had the rest of the day to come up with a sale.

That afternoon, she grew more despondent. The hours were ticking by. When her phone rang, she eagerly picked it up.

"Gabby, you're just the person I want to talk to. This is Robin Woods. You know the young couple you were talking to this morning? Grant and Susie Miller? Grant is the son of a friend of mine, Marjorie Miller. She just talked to him, and she's going to help them buy the SUV you showed them, just like mine."

"Oh, Robin," Gabby gushed. "That's spectacular. Can they come in today? It's the last day of the contest."

"I'll call her now to let her know," said Robin. "I was so impressed that a woman was outselling a man in what is usually a man's business that I was determined to find more sales for you. Bill still can't get over the fact that the two of us made a deal so quickly, so easily. Truth is, he likes to spend time going around to dealerships, talking with the guys. Me? I just want to buy a car. And so does my friend. She's financially secure, so it shouldn't be a problem. She and Grant are going to surprise Susie."

"That's the sweetest thing. I'm so happy to help them. I'll be right here waiting for them. I'll start getting the paperwork ready. Thanks, Robin, for helping me. I might be able to go on this cruise after all."

"I hope so. I'll talk to you later."

Around thirty minutes later, a pleasant-looking, gray-haired woman walked into the dealership with Grant Miller. Gabby hurried over to greet them, surprising Hank, who stood up and looked as if he was going to head their way.

"Grant, it's so nice to see you again. And this must be your mother, Marjorie. Hi, I'm Gabby Willetts, here to help you."

Marjorie shook the hand she'd offered. "Hi, Gabby. Robin Woods has told me all about you. Let's get this done so you can win that cruise you want."

Bursting with excitement, Gabby led the way to her office, ignoring Hank's frowns. The contest was down to the last few hours.

An hour and a half later, the paperwork was done with the understanding that Grant would pick up the car the next day.

Grant stood and shook Gabby's hand. "Susie is going to be so surprised. She thinks I'm helping Mom buy a new lawnmower."

"It's a lovely gesture on your mother's part to help you do this," Gabby said.

Marjorie spoke up. "I'm very excited about their baby. He's my first grandchild, and I want him and his parents to be protected in a safe, reliable car that can handle the space for all the required gear these days."

"You've made an excellent choice." Gabby walked them to the door, thanked them again, and turned around, letting out a long sigh.

"Whoa! What just happened there? You didn't get the sale?" Hank came over to her. "Looks like I might win."

"Actually," she said calmly. "I did get the sale. They'll pick up the car tomorrow."

"Oh, well, that shouldn't count," said Hank. "The sale hasn't gone through until the car is off the lot."

"Of course, it counts," she replied, trying to hide her dismay. "Just because you didn't get a sale from that couple this morning, you can't try to take one away from me."

Dan approached them. "Problems?"

"Gabby is trying to say she made a sale when the car is still on the lot," said Hank.

"I sold it, Dan, but I promised to have it washed and gassed up tomorrow," Gabby said. "It's a surprise for Grant's pregnant wife."

"Sounds like a sale to me," said Dan. "You got all the paperwork for me?"

"Signed and sealed," said Gabby.

"But not delivered," Hank said, checking his watch.

"I'll talk to the powers that be, and we'll announce a winner tomorrow at our regular staff meeting," said Dan.

"Until then, nothing can be done. It's time to close. Now, shake hands on it."

Hank offered his hand, and Gabby took it. At the jolt of what felt like lightning, Gabby fought for control as shock waves traveled from her fingers up her arm and into her body. She turned away. No way did she want Hank to suspect what had happened. She told herself the shock was nothing more than electricity formed when his feet crossed the carpet.

⚓

At home that evening, Gabby went through her closet looking for suitable things to wear on a cruise. If she did win, she'd have to do some shopping. Since moving to Ellenton, she hadn't bought much of anything new. None of it exciting.

She thought of Hank. He was a nice guy, but he wasn't used to the competition. It would do him good to have her win.

⚓

The next morning, Gabby couldn't wait to get to work.

She entered the meeting room at the dealership and looked around for Hank. He was talking to the financial manager, a nice older man named Rick.

"We're rooting for you," said one of the mechanics, giving her a thumbs up.

"Thanks," Gabby said. She took a seat in the front of the room so she could keep an eye on Hank. Studying him, she saw no expression of triumph, just a furrowed brow. She took a moment longer. He certainly was a handsome man. Fit too. The way she'd reacted to his handshake was weird because she had no intention of getting involved with anyone at work. That usually caused nothing but trouble, and she liked her job.

Dan walked into the room and stood in front of the chairs lined up classroom-style. "Glad to see everyone here bright and early. Today, we have a lot to talk about. But first, I have an announcement to make. As you may know, the salesperson with the most sales will win two tickets for a ten-day Caribbean cruise. While several salespeople were involved, two people were the main competitors from the beginning. Gabby and Hank both worked hard for the prize, but at the last minute, one has emerged as the winner. I'm pleased to announce that Gabby has won the cruise."

Amid applause and whistles, Gabby got to her feet and accepted the envelope Dan held out to her.

"It was a fair fight," said Dan, "and I'm proud of the work you did. You deserve this, Gabby."

"Thanks," she said. "I love working here."

"And we love having you," said Dan quietly.

Gabby sat through the rest of the meeting in a daze. She couldn't wait to call Jess in New York to invite her on the cruise. It would be a great girls' getaway.

After the meeting, Hank approached her. "Congratulations, Gabby. Next time, I'll fight even harder. Just what is your magic?"

She smiled. It was so simple. All he had to do was listen to both people in any couple.

"We'll talk later," she said. "I've got to call my friend."

"Okay. *Bon Voyage* or whatever I should say." He gave her a salute and walked away.

She watched him leave and went to the privacy of her office.

There, she opened the envelope, stared at the tickets, and let out a squeal of delight.

Chapter One

Gabby closed the door to her office to call Jessica. She and Jess had been friends since kindergarten and had even decided to become roommates in New York City when Gabby moved there after college graduation. Now that Gabby had relocated to upstate New York, they didn't see each other that often, so a cruise would be a glorious way for them to spend time together.

When Gabby heard Jess's voice, she could scarcely get the words out in her excitement. "Jess! Jess! You know that Caribbean Cruise I was trying to win?"

"The one where you were facing off with the boss's son?"

"The very one. I'm holding the tickets in my hand. We're going to the Caribbean!"

Jess shrieked, "Oh, my God! You did it. That's terrific! I can't wait! When are we leaving?"

Excitement swelled inside her all over again. "We

leave in two weeks. That will give us time to get ready. I want to come to the city to buy some cruising clothes and a new bikini."

"You'd better make it this weekend. We don't have much time. Oh, Gabby, I'm so excited. Work has been awful, and I need a break."

"Okay, I'll see you on Sunday. I have to work Saturday, but if I can leave work early, I'll come down then."

"Wonderful. Can't wait," trilled Jessica before she ended the call.

Gabby sat back in her desk chair, enjoying the feeling of pride that washed through her. Dan was right. She'd worked hard for this prize, and she was going to enjoy it. She looked up as a young man entered the dealership. She expected Hank to make a rush to greet him. But when he didn't, she picked up her small notepad and went to introduce herself.

Later, after leaving her prospective client her business card and the promise to work with him on a satisfying deal, Gabby headed back to her office. If her instincts were right, a call from him tomorrow would help seal a deal. She understood some people needed time to arrive at a decision.

Gabby checked Hank's office, but he wasn't there.

She was sitting in her office going over inventory sheets when Hank strolled in. "I've got a deal for you, Gabby. When I told Ashley you'd won, not me, she cried. She told me she'd already planned her wardrobe for the trip, and she needed us to have this time together."

"I'm sorry, but what does that have to do with me?"

Gabby said, even as a thread of understanding wove through her.

"I'll pay you for those tickets, plus a bonus. Ashley thought the trip was a given and had already planned on it, and I wouldn't mind the trip myself."

Gabby held up her hand to stop him. "I won these fairly, and I intend to use them. My friend and I are very excited about it."

"Okay, as you said, you won them fair and square," said Hank. He gave her a sheepish grin. "You can't blame me for trying."

After he left, Gabby shook her head. She'd known Ashley from high school and was well aware of her persistence in getting her way. One thing was for sure. If Ashley ever manipulated a cruise with Hank, she didn't want it to be aboard the same ship. Gabby could already imagine the many complaints Ashley would have and how she'd find a way to ruin the cruise for Jess and her.

At home, Gabby made a list of the clothing she wanted to buy for the cruise. She'd mentioned a new bikini to Jess, but she needed to add a coverup to wear over it. A fancy sundress for dinner aboard the ship, new sandals, and a couple of cotton tops should do it, she thought happily. Since moving to Ellenton, she'd bought plenty of casual clothes to wear when she wasn't at work.

The next couple of days flew by, and then on Sunday morning, Gabby made her way into the city. She'd hate to admit it, but after living in the suburbs, New York was a little inhibiting as she wended her way through aggressive drivers to find a parking space near her old apartment.

She no sooner had parked and gotten out of her car when Jess appeared. Holding out her arms, she hugged Gabby to her. "I'm so excited. Come on up. I've checked out some of the sales going on. I think we can pick up some great buys." Her green eyes shone with happiness. Jess was always full of excitement, making her curly red hair seem a natural fit for someone so full of life.

Gabby picked up her overnight bag and followed Jess inside the building to the third floor.

"How does it feel to be back in the big city?" Jess asked her. "It's been over a month since we've seen each other and a couple of months since you've been here."

"It's nice to be in the city, but I love the woods around my townhouse and the slower pace of Ellenton," admitted Gabby. She laughed. "Do I sound like an old fogey?"

Jess turned to her, gave her an inspection from head to toe, and said, "With that body and face, you're definitely not that. We're going to have a boatload of fun on that ship."

Jess could always make her laugh.

"Let's get you settled in my room, grab a cup of coffee and a croissant at the coffee shop downstairs, and head out," said Jess, always the planner. "We'll get lunch on the fly and decide what we want to do for dinner later. I'm glad you don't have to work tomorrow. That gives us a full day today."

"It'll be nice to have dinner in the city. That's one thing I miss—being able to walk within a few blocks to find whatever food I want in a variety of restaurants," said Gabby. She set down her overnight bag in Jess's room and turned to her. "Let's go."

They made their way to Fifth Avenue, where they began a systematic inspection of the sales going on inside several stores. This way of shopping wasn't for everyone, but Gabby and Jess were able quickly to tell whether spending time at a place was worth it. And in those that held a lot of promise, they carefully went through the stock to determine if they wanted to make a purchase.

Some of the stores had their cruise and resort wear already on sale. Those were the areas that Gabby liked best. Among other things, she was able to pick up a white-eyelet sleeveless dress perfect for dining aboard the ship and a flowery shift to wear over a bathing suit.

By late lunchtime, both Gabby and Jess were ready to sit and take a rest. They ate at a Thai restaurant, keeping their purchases close by so they could peek inside to view their treasures.

"It's been too long since we've had a real shopping day," said Jess. "This has been fun."

"It's work, but well worth it," said Gabby, totaling up her expenses in her mind. Ashley had made fun of her clothes in high school, but Gabby knew she wouldn't spend her money foolishly no matter how much she loved nice clothes.

"Tell me again about Hank. You haven't talked about him much before now," said Jess giving her a mischievous grin. "I looked up his photo online, and he's really hot. Guess he was a few years ahead of us in school."

"He lived with his mother growing up and was away at high school and then at college," said Gabby. "He's a good-looking guy, for sure, but I don't understand what he sees in Ashley. She hasn't changed much since our high school days. He's disappointed he didn't win the tickets and offered to buy them from me after Ashley made a fuss. She thought it was a done deal that they'd go on the cruise."

Jess made a face. "Don't worry. Ashley will somehow come out a winner. Wait and see. She always gets her way."

Gabby felt the blood rush to her cheeks. "She'd better not mess up our trip."

"How could she? You're not going to sell your tickets. Besides, I can't see the dealership letting both you and Hank go on vacation at the same time."

"I guess," said Gabby, still upset by the idea that Ashley could somehow ruin the trip of a lifetime. The contest prize even included upgraded stateroom accommodations.

They finished their lunch and then stopped at the last few stores on their list before heading back to the apartment. Gabby was glad she'd worn comfortable sneakers. There was fashion, and there was practicality. She'd learned early on to know the difference when traveling the streets of New York.

Gabby kicked off her sneakers at the apartment and plopped down on the couch. Shopping bags surrounded her. She gazed at them with satisfaction, mentally noting the bargains she'd found, especially the white-eyelet sheath and coverup that were her favorites.

"Seems like old times," said Jess, folding herself into a comfy chair nearby. "Can't wait until we can wear all our "sunshine" clothes. I've needed this boost. It's been over a year and a half since I broke up with Mark."

"Mark was never the right man for you," said Gabby quietly. "I'm hoping this cruise will allow you to have fun and forget demeaning guys like him even exist. It's time to move on."

"You're right. I've gone over that past relationship a thousand times in my mind. You aren't the only one who didn't like Mark. I just didn't see him for the kind of guy he was. Promise me that if I ever think of falling in love again, you'll let me know if you think he's wrong for me."

Gabby raised her right hand. "I promise."

"I'm ready for a cup of hot tea and more girl talk," said Jess getting to her feet. "I want all the scoop on everyone in town." Though Jess had grown up in Ellenton, her parents had moved to Florida, so she didn't need to return for visits other than to see Gabby.

Gabby went into the kitchen, or what passed as a kitchen with its small galley design. They fixed themselves cups of tea and went back to the living room, where Gabby did her best to come up with any news of interest.

"Ashley is desperate to get married," Jess commented. "Having one younger sister married and expecting a baby and another about to be married is enough to put pressure on any big sister."

"I've seen her in action around Hank, and I know all that sweetness is fake, but he doesn't see through it. But then, he's a pretty straight-up guy, an honest one. We may face off against one another, but I trust him not to do anything unscrupulous. That's one reason I was so excited to win. It was a fair fight."

"Strangely, I've never met him, but I like what you tell me about Hank. Are you sure you're not interested in him?"

With the memory of the way her body had reacted to his handshake running through her mind, Gabby remained silent, struggling for something to say. "You know it's not wise to mix business with a relationship. Even though I admire him, I recognize that Ashley has her claws into him and isn't about to let anyone else interfere. She's beautiful and smart. Just not very nice. But that's something she keeps well-hidden when she's around him."

"Well, like you said, it's not wise to mix love and work. Don't I know it," said Jess with a sigh. "I never should have been with Mark when we were working in the same office.

"Let's watch some romantic movies and eat in," Gabby suggested.

"Perfect," Jess said. "Is Chinese food okay?"

"Sounds perfect. Like a lot of other evenings we've spent together between dates."

"Who knows? We may meet the loves of our life aboard our ship, Tropical Magic."

Gabby smiled. "I do love the name."

Chapter Two

Back home, Gabby settled into a routine of working hard and marking the days off her calendar. Dan had talked to her about a possible new position in the future. He didn't say more, and Gabby didn't want to pursue it until she returned from the cruise.

At last, the time came for her to head to New York to Jess's apartment. From there, they'd take a cab to Kennedy Airport for the flight to Fort Lauderdale and Port Everglades. Gabby had done some traveling, but this would be her first cruise. As she drove her car into the city, her excitement grew.

Jess greeted her at her door wearing a big floppy straw hat. "I've been practicing saying '*Bon Voyage*' in the mirror, and I like the sound of it."

Gabby laughed. "The day is finally here." She stepped inside and stared aghast at the two large suitcases, canvas carry-on bag, and big purse Jess had sitting on the floor.

"What's wrong?" Jess asked her.

"Are you really taking both of those suitcases? The ship warned of bringing too much luggage."

"You know me. I want to be prepared for anything. Besides, your small bag will make up the difference," said Jess, winking at her.

Gabby laughed. She wasn't going to let tiny details worry her.

Aboard the plane, Gabby took a deep breath. She needed this vacation. The past year and a half had been difficult with her father's illness and passing, a move out of the family home into a townhouse, and the start of a new job. She turned to Jess, who had her Kindle in her hands. "What are you reading?"

Jess grinned. "Something I saw online and had to buy. A shipboard romance story."

Gabby elbowed her. "Trying to pick up ideas?"

Jess shrugged. "Can't hurt, can it?"

They laughed together, and then Gabby stared out the window of the plane. They flew through patches of floating clouds that covered the ground below in shadows before giving way to sunshine.

When they arrived at the airport, signs led them to the buses that would carry them to Port Everglades.

The port was much larger than Gabby had thought but was well organized. The bus driver dropped them off near a pier where the ship was berthed. There, Gabby and Jess were met by porters who tagged and labeled their luggage before joining the line of other passengers going through security.

At check-in Gabby showed her proof of citizenship, had her picture taken, and was issued a cruise ID card, charge card, and stateroom key.

Walking the gangway onto the ship, Gabby held her breath, savoring the moment.

A smiling female crew member wearing navy pants and a crisp white blouse greeted her warmly, checked her ticket and ID, and said, "Welcome aboard. You have a lovely VIP room assigned to you on deck #12. Enjoy. Your luggage will be delivered to your room." She indicated behind her. "The elevators are beyond us. Here is an extra map of the ship. An attendant is by the elevators to help guide you should you need it."

"Thanks," Gabby said. "I can find my way." Stepping into the interior felt like entering a glamorous hotel. She couldn't wait to explore it.

"This is even more luxurious than the pictures showed," said Jess walking behind her. "I can't wait to see our suite."

They rode to deck #12. Their suite was on the starboard side, which meant they could see sunsets as they cruised south.

Inside, the suite contained two twin beds, a pull-out couch, a small desk, a sitting area, and, best of all, a balcony with two chairs.

"I'm surprised how spacious it feels," Jess said. "And look how much storage space it has. I'm happy I brought as many clothes as I did. There's room for all of it."

Gabby cocked an eyebrow at her. "Better leave me my share of space."

Jess gave her a teasing grin. "It's a good thing you didn't bring a lot."

"I'm going out to the balcony and take a look," said Gabby. She unlocked and opened the sliding door and stepped outside. The world opened up to her like a panorama.

"Oh, it's going to be so beautiful," gushed Jess. She clapped her hands. "Thank you, thank you, for being such a terrific saleswoman, Gabby. I love you."

Gabby laughed when Jess threw her arms around her. They were more like sisters than friends. It felt fabulous to be able to do something like this for her.

A knock at the door caught Gabby's attention. She opened it to find a male staff member.

"Hi, I'm Ricardo, your cabin steward. May I show you the amenities of the room or bring you some ice?"

Jess joined them, and both she and Gabby stared at the handsome, dark-haired man whose shiny dark eyes were full of mischief. "I need also to tell you where your muster station is located. If you haven't seen it yet, the map on the back of your stateroom door will show you."

"I'd love some ice," said Jess, batting her eyes at Ricardo.

"Let me get the ice bucket. I'll fill it and bring it right back," he said, winking at Jess.

After he left, Jess turned to Gabby. "Oh, I'm going to have so much fun!"

Ricardo returned, described some of the amenities, and left with a request for them to go to the 30-minute muster drill where they'd be told where they should go in the unlikely event of an emergency. The ship wouldn't leave port until all passengers had received the drill. Only then would the sailaway party begin on deck.

They'd been assigned a muster station near one of the lifeboats. When they arrived, several other passengers were already gathered in their spot wearing life jackets like Gabby and Jess. A crew member explained that this is where they should go should they hear the distress signal. They had to listen to more safety measures and instructions, and then they were ready to go.

Gabby could hardly wait to start celebrating. They hurried back to their room to leave their life jackets and change their clothes.

"Ready to go?" said Jess, wearing shorts and a tank top.

"Better grab a sweater in case a breeze comes up," said Gabby.

"Got mine," said Jess after rummaging through a drawer. "Let's go. I can taste a margarita already. Then I'll feel as if I'm on a tropical vacation."

"Easy, girl," said Gabby laughing. "We've got ten days ahead of us."

Gabby and Jess headed for the sailaway party in full swing on the main deck. People from all over the boat were gathering to celebrate the ship's departure. Staff members handed out margaritas, and Gabby and Jess each snatched a drink.

Jess grabbed Gabby's arm. "Let's move away from the horns. A woman at work warned me about them as the ship departed."

They moved to a place along the rail and looked out at the welcoming sea.

"Here's to us and a wonderful cruise," said Jess, lifting her glass.

Smiling, Gabby lifted hers. "To us!"

She'd just taken a sip of her margarita when she noticed movement farther down the rail. She choked and tried to catch her breath.

Startled, Jess rubbed her back. "Are you all right, Gabby?"

Unable to speak, Gabby turned to look behind her.

What is it?" Jess said. "I don't see anything wrong."

Gabby drew in a deep breath and scanned the area again. "I swear I saw Hank."

"Let's just forget work and enjoy ourselves," said Jess. "C'mon, the band is playing. Let's dance. I'm ready for this."

Telling herself that Jess was right, she had to let loose and enjoy herself, Gabby followed Jess.

After a workout on the dance floor, Gabby accepted another margarita and returned to the ship's rail, where she and Jess could get a clear view of the ship's departure. Down below, people stood waving at them.

Gabby scanned the passengers around her. When she saw no sign of Hank, she sighed happily and stared out at the water. The ship's horns blew, and a loud cheer went up from the crowd on deck.

Goosepimples traveled down Gabby's back. They were on their way.

She and Jess embraced, and that's when she saw her.

Gabby jerked away from Jess and stared at Ashley and Hank, who were hugging a distance away from her. As she neared them, there was no mistaking Hank's butterscotch hair, his broad shoulders, his cute butt. Beside him, Ashley was wearing white pants and a blue and white striped sailor-style top—one of the expensive outfits she and Jess had seen in one of the stores on their shopping spree.

Jess took hold of her shoulder. "Hey! What are you staring at?"

"It's Ashley. She's here with Hank."

"Oh, no," Jess groaned. "That's trouble for sure."

"Exactly," said Gabby, unable to hold in her dismay. The last thing she needed on this "let loose, maybe find romance" vacation was discovering Ashley aboard the ship. But she moved forward to greet them.

Hank looked up, saw her, and smiled. "Surprise!"

"It certainly is." Jess walked up beside her, giving her moral support.

Gabby turned to her and back to Hank. "This is my friend, Jessica Knight." Gabby's voice lowered. "Ashley, you may remember Jess from high school." Ashley and her friends had tormented Jess for her size and red hair.

"I certainly remember you, Ashley," said Jess, her voice as cold as the ice in their celebratory drinks. "You and those awful friends of yours."

Hank glanced from Jess to Ashley. Though he

remained quiet, Gabby knew from his expression that he was disturbed by Jess's revelation.

"What are you doing here? Who's taking care of the dealership at home?" asked Gabby.

"Dad knew how bad Ashley and I wanted this cruise, and he suggested we come. He thought it might be a wise idea if a couple of other salespeople had some time to shine with both of us away so they could practice their skills."

Gabby frowned. "He did?"

"This cruise is a promise Hank made to me," said Ashley. "You may have thought you won the contest fair and square, but I heard all about how you got your customers to call friends of theirs and other tricks during the final days."

Gabby studied Hank. "Really?"

"I never said anything like that." Hank looked miserable. Gabby almost felt sorry for him as they stared at one another. Almost.

As they walked away, Jess spoke quietly into Gabby's ear, "What's with the way Hank kept looking at you? Gabby, you're holding out on me."

Gabby stopped and stared at Jess. "Are you crazy? What are you talking about? Hank is someone I work with, compete with. Nothing more. And right now, I'm so upset I could cry. You know Ashley is going to find a way to make things difficult for us."

"Let's forget the two of them and have fun looking around for a bit," said Jess. "Our dinner is at seven, and I can't wait to meet the couple we're dining with."

Gabby looped her arm around Jess's, and they headed up to the Lido deck.

There, on the upper deck, the sun was shining on the large pool's surface, sending glittering beams of light around it. Sunchairs were lined up around the pool in four rows, giving room to many sunbathers. Several spas were located near the pool. A poolside restaurant with offerings of hamburgers, hotdogs, and similar fare sat at one end of the pool area, and a huge outdoor projection screen dominated the other end, no doubt for movie nights. On a higher level, a huge water slide reached for the sky.

"Looks like this is the playground," said Jess. "But I'm not sure about that water slide. It's so high up in the air."

"Yeah, I'm not so sure about it either." Gabby walked over to the railing and looked out. From here, she studied the horizon, delighted by the view of the open sea in front of her. She breathed in the fresh air and let out a long breath. This cruise is what she needed, and no one was going to take its pleasure away from her. Not even Ashley or Hank.

Chapter Three

In their cabin, Gabby and Jess took their time changing for dinner, spending lots of moments on the balcony of their stateroom.

Gabby put on the white-eyelet sundress she'd bought and took a seat outside. Jess always took longer to get ready for events than Gabby, and, for once, Gabby was glad. She wanted time to sit alone and take in the view.

She was startled when she felt movement behind her and turned in her chair to see Hank step out onto his balcony.

Gabby's heart sank. She got to her feet.

Hank's eyes widened when he saw her. "Gabby, I didn't realize you were right next door. We signed up for a balcony stateroom but didn't know if we could make the cruise until the last moment when this stateroom became available."

"Let's just ignore one another as much as we can," said Gabby. "Try not to interfere with me, and I'll try to stay out of your way."

Hank gave her an apologetic look. "I'm sorry, Gabby. As I said, I didn't know we'd be this close. And I never discussed you stealing away sales or anything like that. I don't know why Ashley said that."

"Who are you talking to?" Jess asked, joining Gabby.

Silent, Gabby simply pointed to Hank.

Jesse stared at Hank and then shook her head. "You've got to be freaking kidding me."

"We're going to avoid each other as much as possible," Gabby said.

Jess's lips thinned as she faced Hank. "You'd better not be eating dinner with us."

"If you're heading to dinner now, then we're not. We have a later time."

"Thank God for small favors," Jess muttered. "Are you ready, Gabby? Let's go before Ashley appears and ruins my appetite."

Hank's eyebrows rose.

"Unless a miracle has happened, Ashley is not someone I want to be with," said Jess eying Hank. "You'll find out what I'm talking about."

"See you, or not," said Gabby. She gave Hank a wave as she entered her stateroom and slid the glass door closed behind her.

"Of all the rotten luck," said Jess.

"I couldn't believe it when I first saw him," said Gabby. "But I don't want anything to ruin our vacation."

Jess bobbed her head. "You're right. Let's go and enjoy dinner."

⚓

Gabby stood a moment at the entrance to the dining room. Several crystal ceiling chandeliers shed light below to the tables covered with crisp, white-linen cloths. The bold floral patterns on the dark-green carpeting lent a tropical feel to the space. In addition to the main floor of dining tables, a balcony above held tables next to windows.

Nearby, a staff member greeted passengers. Gabby showed her ID to him, and he pointed to a spot on the balcony above them. "Take the stairs to that level, and you'll easily find your table. Your tablemates are already there."

Curious to see who'd they be sharing meals with, Gabby headed up the stairway with Jess.

As they approached the table, Gabby stared at an older woman with short gray hair and a handsome, gray-haired man sitting beside her.

They looked up as Gabby and Jess drew near.

Even though a nearby waiter rushed to seat them, the man scrambled to his feet.

"How nice that we are with two young, beautiful women to share a meal," said the woman. She held out her hand. "You're about my granddaughters' ages, and we enjoy them so much. I'm Eleanor Rizzo, but please call me Ellie."

"And I'm John," the man said, giving them a wide smile.

After handshakes and greetings had been exchanged and both Gabby and Jess were seated, the waiter asked if he could bring them something to drink.

"Why don't you share our bottle of wine?" Ellie said. "It's a lovely Italian Barolo. We visited the winery two years ago."

"How nice," said Gabby. "I recognize a delicious wine when I taste it, but I don't know much about them. This will be an excellent way to learn."

Ellie turned to John. "John is a connoisseur of wines after being in the restaurant and inn business for years."

"An inn? How exciting!" exclaimed Jess.

"What's your cooking specialty?" Gabby asked, studying the man who had a twinkle in his eye.

He grinned. "Italian recipes from my grandmother were the favorites at the restaurant. Having Ellie as my business partner was another smart move."

"You worked together?" said Gabby. "Isn't that difficult?"

"It takes a lot of compromises," admitted Ellie.

"How long have you two been married?" Jess asked.

Ellie and John looked at one another and laughed. "Almost three years," Ellie said, still chuckling. "It's a long story. John and I have been together for many more years than that."

"Whatever you've done, I can see that it's working," said Gabby.

"I hope to find a man like you've found," said Jess, her voice wistful.

Ellie sat straighter and gave Jess a steady look. "Tell me a little bit about yourself."

Jess told her about her job in New York, her family, and how she knew Gabby. "I'm hoping to find romance aboard this ship. Someone different from my friends back home."

"And how about you, Gabby?" Ellie said.

Gabby told her about coming back to her hometown to take care of her father and her job at the dealership.

"Too bad the guy she competes with is here on the boat with a woman we both detest. Especially because I think he has a thing for Gabby."

"I see," said Ellie, studying them both. "I'll keep my eyes open ..."

John placed a hand on Ellie's arm. "Now, Ellie," he warned.

"Don't worry about me," Ellie said. She faced Gabby and Jess. "My friends and I at Sanderling Cove in Florida matched up our grandkids, and now my three grand-daughters are happily married. We just seem to know when something is right."

"But you're done with all that. Right, Ellie?" said John giving her a stern look.

Ellie smiled impishly. "You never can tell."

Their waiter approached to tell them about the specials, and conversation turned to their meals. But Gabby remained amused by her dinner partners. They were adorable together.

After dinner, Ellie said, "Are you two going to the show? They say it's a wonderful one. A revue of Broadway hits."

"We thought we would see it and then maybe listen to the band on the Lido deck," Gabby answered.

"I'm going to the casino," John announced.

Ellie frowned. "Guess I'll go alone to the show."

"Why don't you join us?" said Jess. "We'd love to spend more time with you."

Ellie's face lit. "You mean it? I'd love to, but I don't want to interfere with your plans. How can you meet men if you're stuck with an old lady like me?"

Gabby and Jess laughed together. Ellie was such easy company they felt like friends already.

While John headed in one direction, Gabby, Jess, and Ellie headed in another.

"Don't let John's discouragement bother you. I know what I'm doing when it comes to putting people together," said Ellie. "It comes from working for years at our inn. You develop an instinct about these things."

"Well, if you see someone I ought to meet, just make it happen," said Jess, giving Ellie a teasing smile.

"As a matter of fact, I met a young man while standing in line to board the ship," said Ellie. "He's here as a favor to his grandmother. Let me do more investigation, and I'll let you know."

Gabby and Jess exchanged amused looks.

The show was fun and filled with talented singers and dancers. Gabby loved shows in New York and thought this one was as good as some she'd seen.

"Thanks for keeping me company," said Ellie. "I'm going to head back to my stateroom. Enjoy the rest of the evening."

Gabby and Jess said goodbye to her and went up to

the Lido deck for something to drink and to listen to the band under the stars.

When they arrived on deck, Jess announced she wanted to walk around a bit to check the place out.

Gabby found a table midship and sat down, pleased by the view. Above her, stars twinkled in the dark sky while the rolling waves below reflected what light they could in the black expanse of water.

"There you are," came a voice Gabby instantly recognized. She turned to find Hank standing nearby.

"Yes?" Gabby said, wondering how to respond. She looked for Ashley but didn't see her.

"May I sit?" Hank asked.

"Where's Ashley?" Gabby said in response.

"She's not feeling well and went to lie down in the cabin."

Gabby waved him to a seat and observed him quietly as he took it.

He turned to her. "I want to apologize again. To keep my word to Ashley about going on a cruise, I tried to make reservations on this boat, thinking it wouldn't work. Then I got a call that a suite came available and everything happened so quickly that I didn't give you enough consideration. I kept thinking a boat with several thousand passengers would make it easy to avoid seeing you."

Gabby sighed. "To be truthful, it wouldn't be so difficult if you were with someone other than Ashley. You heard Jess. She still has issues with her."

"And you?" Hank asked, giving her a steady look demanding an honest answer.

"Ashley has a way of putting on a pleasant front, but I

know what kind of person she is. She's been very hurtful to me and others. Sooner or later, that mean streak will come out."

Hank nodded thoughtfully. "I appreciate your honesty. I haven't been in town that long, just a little over a year, like you. And I didn't grow up there, so I have no background information on some of the local people. I've begun to suspect that what you're telling me is true. She doesn't like the word 'no.'"

"She thinks she's entitled to this cruise," said Gabby.

"I'm having serious second thoughts about her. The odd thing is my father encouraged me to make the trip. Weird, huh?"

"Yes," said Gabby. Dan Davis was a shrewd man. Why would he push something like this when she knew he didn't care for Ashley? Then it hit her. Dan wanted Hank to discover for himself what others already thought of his girlfriend. It was something Hank would have to find out for himself.

A waitress appeared. "Can I bring you something?"

Hank turned to Gabby. "What'll you have?"

"I'd like a virgin fruit punch," said Gabby. "With lots of ice, please."

"And I'll have an IPA," Hank said. "I'm still getting used to this heat and humidity."

The waitress gave him a brilliant smile, flirting with him. "Nice choice. Have fun you two."

"Where's your friend?" Hank asked.

Gabby frowned. "I don't know. She was going to walk around for a bit. She probably met someone to talk to. We have the best tablemates for dinner. A darling older couple."

"Ashley felt too sick to go to dinner, so I just had a burger and fries. Not too exciting, but they tasted delicious."

"The buffet is still open," Gabby said.

"Yeah, I thought I'd go there after this. I'm glad I saw you, Gabby. I'll try to stay out of your way."

Their drinks came.

"Here's to a great cruise," said Hank, tapping his bottle against her glass of punch.

"Yes, for each of us," Gabby said, smiling at him.

He paused, settled his gaze on her, and then rose. "Thanks for the talk. "

Gabby watched him walk away and told her heart to slow down. That look he gave her was more than friendly, and she wasn't certain how she felt about it.

Jess appeared, accompanied by a very handsome black man. "Gabby, I want you to meet Sam. Dr. Samuel Johnson. He's here on the cruise to help take care of his grandmother."

Gabby turned to Sam. Friendly brown eyes met hers as a smile turned up the corner of his lips. Gabby felt herself being drawn to his calm demeanor.

When Gabby learned Sam was a doctor who'd recently set up practice in New York City, she was even more attracted to the idea of Jess and him being together. The pink flush on Jess's cheeks, the shine in her eyes, and the way she kept looking at Sam told her Jess was smitten in a way Gabby hadn't ever seen. When it became apparent that Gabby was nothing more than an onlooker to the glances between Jess and Sam and no real part of their conversation, Gabby excused herself. It had been a long day.

Back in her room, she stepped out onto the balcony and sat in a chair. The moon was out, and she wanted a moment alone to relish being aboard the ship on a wonderful prepaid trip. She'd worked hard for the winning tickets. She'd also proved to herself how much she loved her job and her new life in Ellenton.

She felt rather than saw a presence nearby and looked across to the balcony next to her. She recognized the shape of a man sitting in a chair and silently watched as he turned to face her.

"Nice night, huh?" said Hank.

"A perfect time to sit and enjoy the beauty of it. Did you make it to the buffet?" she asked.

"Yeah. They put on quite a spread. You'll have to try it sometime."

"I intend to," Gabby said and stood. "'Night, Hank."

She went inside, closed the sliding door, and pulled the drapes shut. She got ready for bed and then slid under the sheet and blanket and stretched out. There was something about the sea air that made her feel so relaxed.

Sometime later, she stirred in her sleep and saw Jess slide into the twin bed opposite hers.

"How did it go?" Gabby murmured.

"I know it's going to sound crazy, but I think I'm in

love," Jess said. "We talked and talked. He's a fantastic person, so easy to be with."

Gabby sat up and stared at the bedside clock. Two A. M. "I'm glad, Jess, but this is only the first day of the cruise. Be careful."

"I know," Jess murmured. "I can't quite believe it."

Chapter Four

The next morning, Gabby and Jess made their way to the main dining room for breakfast. They'd have a choice of food to eat in a variety of places throughout the day, but Gabby wanted to eat breakfast in a quieter place.

When they found their way to their table, she was pleasantly surprised to see Ellie and John sitting there.

"Do you mind if we join you?" Gabby asked.

"Not at all," said Ellie. "I'm happy to see you. I have more information on the young man I wanted you to meet, Jess. He's a doctor in New York City, which would be perfect for you. He's traveling with his grandmother to help her, which tells you what kind of man he is …"

Jess cut her off. "Are you talking about Sam Johnson?"

Ellie's look of surprise was cute to see. "Why, yes. Do you know him?"

"Actually, he and I met last night and have hit it off," said Jess, her lips curving into a smile no one could miss.

"Well, then, I guess my instincts are still spot on. That makes me happy," said Ellie. She faced Gabby. "Anyone of interest for you on the ship?"

Gabby shook her head. "I'm just going to enjoy being here, getting some overdue rest, and having fun."

"We'll see," said Ellie, winking at her.

Gabby couldn't help laughing. Ellie was so full of life.

After breakfast, Gabby and Jess decided to get some poolside sun. Sitting by the pool was a nice way to start the day.

They found lounge chairs in the last row, away from the pool. They'd just taken their seats when Jess sat up and waved. Sam headed toward them from behind a wheelchair holding an older woman. At closer range, Gabby saw where Sam had gotten his good looks. His grandmother was a lovely-looking woman with cocoa-colored skin and light-brown eyes that seemed to take in everything around her.

"Gran, I want you to meet Jessica Knight and her friend, Gabby Willets." He placed a hand on the woman's shoulder. "This is my grandmother, Arabelle Johnson."

After greetings were exchanged, Sam turned to his grandmother. "Why don't we stay here for a while? Your spa treatment isn't until much later."

Arabelle smiled sweetly. "This is fine. Go enjoy your-self in the pool."

Sam looked at Jess. "Shall we?"

Jess nodded, and they walked to the pool together.

"I see my grandson has his eyes on your friend," Arabelle said to Gabby. "I'm surprised. He hasn't been interested in anyone for a long time. I was giving up hope for him."

"Jess is a good person. I've never seen her this way. She told me she and Sam stayed up late talking."

"I hope no one gets hurt," said Arabelle. "But then, I've been known to be overly protective of the boy. I've raised him since he was a toddler."

"He seems very nice," said Gabby. "I can see why Jess has fallen for him." She looked up as Ellie approached them.

"Hello, again, Arabelle," said Ellie. "It's good to see you out and about. Where's that handsome grandson of yours?" She winked at Gabby. "Guess he and Jess are together."

"Swimming in the pool," said Gabby.

"Do you mind if I join you two?" said Ellie.

"Not at all," Arabelle answered for them both. "I want to know more about that honeymoon trip you and John took through Europe. I haven't been back in years due to the inconvenience of traveling lately."

"If you two don't mind, I'm going to head to the pool myself," said Gabby getting to her feet.

The women waved her off, and Gabby walked away, feeling a little left out. She was approaching the pool when she noticed Hank and Ashley stretched out in chairs. Ashley was wearing a tiny black bikini that showed off her body. Hank was wearing red swim trunks. Her gaze rested on him. Who knew beneath the dress shirts he wore at work that his abs were so muscular? She sighed and went on her way. Jess saw her and waved her over. "Come on in. The water's great."

Sam smiled at her as she joined them. "I see Gran is talking to your dining mate. That Ellie is something else. Just what Gran needs."

"They seem to enjoy one another," said Gabby. "It's hot. I thought I'd have some juice. Want anything, you two?"

"Juice sounds terrific," said Jess.

"Nothing for me," Sam said. "But thanks."

Gabby walked over to the tropical juice stand.

She'd just ordered two drinks when a voice behind her said. "Looks delicious."

She turned and faced Hank. "Another beautiful day. How are you this morning?"

"Fine. Just getting some rays," he responded, taking in her appearance without making her uncomfortable. "Makes it nice when I know it's cold and snowy back home."

Gabby grinned. "True. I'm so glad to be here. Have a fun day."

She left but felt his eyes on her as she walked away.

At the pool, she handed Jess her drink and sat down on the edge of the pool beside her. "Where did Sam go?"

"To check on his grandmother," Jess replied. "You and I are going into San Juan when it's time. Right?"

Gabby nodded happily. "I want to tour Old San Juan."

"Do you mind if Sam joins us?" Jess asked, looking uncertain.

"Not at all," Gabby replied. She didn't want anything to stand between Jess and her new love interest. As different as they appeared to be—her bouncy nature and his quiet steadiness—they seemed so right with one another.

"Thanks," said Jess. "Honestly, I've never felt this way about anyone else. It's like we were meant to be together." She held up a hand. "I know it's been less than twenty-four hours, but I feel as if I've always known him." She frowned. "Do you think we met in a former life?"

Gabby shook her head. "Anything's possible. Just try and take it nice and slow."

But as Sam walked toward them, a broad grin spread across Jess's face.

Gabby studied Sam, but his eyes remained focused on Jess.

At the last minute, Sam had to cancel going into San Juan with them. Gabby and Jess joined the others heading down the gangway and onto the pier. Gabby couldn't wait to find out all she could about the area. From a brochure, she learned that Old San Juan was built in 1521 and is the oldest settlement within Puerto Rico, that El Morro, the fort protecting San Juan against attackers approaching from the sea, was first constructed in 1539 and finished in 1790, and that San Cristobal was built to protect against attacks on San Juan by land.

As interesting as its history, Gabby loved walking in Old San Juan. Some of the cobblestones were blue, cast from furnace slag from iron smelting brought over on Spanish ships as ballast. They toured the Casa Blanca

Museum and the Cathedral of San Juan Bautista and then were ready for a refreshing drink before tackling shopping in the colorful shops lining the streets.

When it came time to board the ship again, Gabby was more than ready to have a swim in the pool and relax before dinner, while Jess went to find Sam.

That evening Jess and Gabby sat with Ellie and John in the dining room, exchanging conversation about their day. Ellie had foregone historical tours in San Juan and spent a few hours checking out the shops, searching for santos—wood carvings of saints—for one of her friends, and just enjoying the atmosphere. John had joined a tour of the Bacardi rum factory as research for the Sanderling Cove Inn.

"Tomorrow should be a fun day," said Ellie. "I've signed up for the snorkeling group. How about you two?"

"I've signed up," said Gabby.

"I've signed up, but if I end up not going, I'll do one of the other snorkeling group tours." Jess gave us a shy smile. "Sam might be busy with his grandmother, and I said I'd wait for him to go snorkeling."

"Arabelle Johnson is a fascinating person, a lovely lady. Her deceased husband, Jerol, was a very well-respected state congressman. She's been disabled only for the last ten years. Multiple Sclerosis. Before then, she was very active with children's programs."

"Arabelle raised him from the time he was young, after his father died in a tragic incident, and Sam was left alone," said Jess. "He never really knew his mother. She took off when he was two."

"Yes, Arabelle told me about that. She's a very strong woman. From what she's said, Sam is strong too, a smart, young, independent man who dotes on her," said Ellie. "I have a feeling about you two..."

At the warning look John gave her, she suddenly stopped talking.

Ellie and John stared at one another silently, then both burst into laughter.

Gabby loved how well they could communicate with or without words.

Dinner was another delicious meal. Gabby chose pan-seared red snapper with a lemon caper sauce that was as elegant as any fish she'd ever tasted. Jess went with a shrimp dish, and both Ellie and John ordered beef filet, simply grilled.

After dinner, Gabby decided to go to the casino with John. She'd never been a gambler, and though John only allowed himself a small amount of money to gamble with, he was eager to show her how to play blackjack.

Jess opted to go with Ellie, who'd made plans to meet Arabelle at the after-dinner show in the theater.

Gabby followed John inside the casino and stared at the slot machines.

"Penny slots are an easy choice," said John. "If you're like me, you don't want to blow all your money at once."

"Right. I've worked too hard to just give it away by

gambling," said Gabby, but she was fascinated by what she saw. She decided to use some change for the slots, but what she really wanted to do was to watch John at a blackjack game. That required thinking, not just pushing buttons to see if you won.

After playing the slots and losing her designated money, she walked over to the blackjack table where John was playing.

She was surprised to see Hank standing there as well.

He grinned at her. "Here to win?"

"Here to learn," she answered, looking for Ashley. "Where's your girlfriend?"

His brow creased and he shook his head. "After a very nasty argument over something stupid, I told Ashley it was over between us. The downside is we have to continue sharing a room, but that's all it is. She enjoyed telling me she already has her eye on someone else, a better catch, a rich doctor from New York City."

A jolt of concern surged through Gabby. "Is the doctor's name Sam by any chance?"

"Yeah. How did you know? They met at the pool this afternoon."

"Just a suspicion, that's all." Gabby felt sick. Was Sam the kind of guy who flirted with everyone? He didn't seem that way. So, what was going on? She excused herself and went to find Jess.

Jess was sitting in the theater with Ellie, Arabelle, and Sam. She waved Jess over to her.

"Come with me. I have to tell you something." Gabby's stomach did a flip-flop inside her. She didn't want to ruin Jess's trip, but she couldn't let her friend get hurt.

"What is it?" Jess asked. "You look upset."

"I am. I just found out that Hank broke up with Ashley, and she already has her eyes on a certain doctor from New York City named Sam."

Jess laughed softly. "I already know. Sam told me about his encounter with Ashley this afternoon while we were ashore. After finding out he was a doctor, she actually told him he could give her a physical exam anytime. Can you believe it?"

"Whew! I thought maybe he was one of those guys who likes to play the field," said Gabby.

"Even after all I've told you about him?" Jess said, frowning.

"I know, I know, but worse things have happened," said Gabby, feeling foolish. "I just don't want to see you hurt."

"Thanks, but I'm fine," Jess said. She studied Gabby. "What are you going to do about Hank? He said he broke it off with Ashley?"

"Yes, he did, and that's the end of it. Hank and I work together. We can be friends, but I can't do anything to jeopardize my job. I like it, and I'm successful. I'm not about to give it up because I'm attracted to Hank. His father has a strict code about not dating people at work. He says he wants to give everyone a fair chance at success."

Jess shrugged. "It's your call. Just wondered. That's all. Want to join us in the theater?"

Gabby shook her head. "No, I think I'll go back and watch John play blackjack. He wants to show me how."

When she entered the casino, she saw John and went over to him. Hank was nowhere in sight. She breathed a sigh of relief and went to the blackjack table.

John spoke softly to her, explaining some of the basics. She watched and listened carefully, and then when the dealer asked if she wanted to play, she surprised herself by saying yes.

Once she got into the game, the noise around her subsided, and she saw only the cards, added numbers in her head, and speculated on what card was coming next.

The dealer grinned at her. "We have a winner. I think we have a real pro here."

Gabby laughed and shook her head. "I'm just learning."

"Okay, let's try again." The dealer dealt cards to her and three other players.

Once more, she concentrated on the cards, figuring in her mind the odds of which number might show up.

"And, ladies and gentlemen, we have a winner again," announced the dealer.

Gabby took a quick bow as people around her clapped, and then she stepped away from the table and bumped into Hank.

"You're fantastic," said Hank. "But I'm not surprised. At work, you're excellent with numbers, and now this. I'd better be careful in the future, or I'll be out of a job."

She laughed. "No chance of that. You're the owner's son."

"I wasn't supposed to say anything yet, but I'm

leaving Lexus and moving to the town next to Ellenton to manage my dad's Mercedes dealership there."

"Oh," said Gabby, her mind racing.

Hank grinned. "Don't worry. We'll still compete against each other. Dad said the two of us bring in a ton of business that way."

"We'll see how that goes," said Gabby, giving him a teasing grin. "You know I don't like to lose."

"And I like to win," Hank said, laughing softly. "I don't know what it is about you, Gabby. You're a nice person, but as you say, you don't like to lose. It makes me want to win even more. You know?"

Gabby nodded. Competing against him for sales was a game, but winning was worth fighting for. She wouldn't even be on this cruise if she didn't believe that.

"Okay, now that we've settled that, want to go up to the Lido deck with me? They have an awesome band."

"Just to be sure, you and Ashley aren't together anymore?" She needed to be clear on that.

"No," said Hank. "I think she's as relieved as I am after seeing some of the other guys aboard the ship and hearing what they do for a living. A car salesman isn't necessarily glamorous."

"I'm sorry that it's happened this way," said Gabby.

"I'm not," said Hank. "My dad never liked the idea of me with Ashley, and after seeing this side of her, I don't like the idea myself. She was a bad move on my part."

"All right then, let's go," said Gabby. "I could use some fresh air. It looks like another beautiful evening under the stars."

On the Lido deck, a band was playing rock music. The thumping beat, keeping time with the rhythm of her heart, filled Gabby with excitement.

Hank found a table alongside the rail where they could look out through the glass at the sea beyond them. The stars twinkled above them. Whimsically, Gabby imagined they were sending sweet wishes to them.

"It's beautiful, huh?" said Hank, taking a seat opposite her.

"Oh, yes. The sky at sea is unbelievable, so all-encompassing. As silly as it might sound, I feel as if I could reach up and touch the moon."

Hank studied her. "I like that."

A waiter appeared, and they each ordered a beer.

They talked easily with one another. Gabby asked Hank about his childhood and why he hadn't grown up in Ellenton, and he was honest with her, telling her about living with his mother and her second husband in Arizona. Though he visited his father during some holidays and summers, his dad was always busy with work, so it made more sense for him to stay in Arizona for the school year and more. After college, he worked for a friend of his stepfather's, but when his dad asked him to come to Ellenton to help with the business, he was ready for a change. He and his dad had grown very close, and though he was fairly new to the area, he liked Ellenton with its four seasons.

Gabby told him about growing up with a single father

and how time spent together had given her a love of cars, which is why she liked her job.

"My dad speaks very highly of your father. Says he was a good man," said Hank, bringing unexpected tears to Gabby's eyes.

He noticed, leaned over, and thumbed a tear off her cheek. "Sorry if I made you sad."

"I still miss him so much. Cancer is a cruel disease," she said.

He gave her a sympathetic look. "I know."

They stared out at the water, and then Hank said, "Hey, the music has changed. Want to dance?"

"Sure," said Gabby, eager to chase away her sadness.

They were among several couples on the dance floor as the melodic music filled the air.

Hank took her in his arms.

She tensed as he pulled her close and then relaxed. It felt so right as they swayed to the music.

Gabby gazed up at the sky and wondered how she could be so lucky to be on this cruise. It was turning out to be much different from what she'd thought and so much better.

Chapter Five

After oversleeping and being too late for breakfast in the dining room, Gabby moved through the buffet on the Lido deck. She told herself it was the sea air that had given her the best sleep she'd had in months. But she knew it was more than that. While Jess was falling in love, Gabby was exploring a friendship with a man she liked. They were comfortable with one another. That made it very easy to relax and enjoy the time they had together on the cruise. She wasn't going to think beyond that.

She was eating her breakfast when she noticed Ashley talking to an attractive man on the nearby pool deck. She observed her pose and wondered if Ashley realized how blatantly sexual it was. But then, Ashley must figure this was the only way to land a suitable rich man. Gabby was happy Hank had finally understood what kind of person his ex-girlfriend was, but she wasn't about to get caught up in any of the drama. She'd continue to be a friend to Hank, but that's all. She had a feeling that by the end of the trip, Ashley would realize her mistake in letting Hank go and want him back.

Gabby enjoyed a moment alone, gazing around at her fellow passengers. Jess had gone for a pedicure, and Gabby was just waiting for the boat tour to Tortola and the snorkeling class she'd signed up for. She noticed Arabelle and saw Sam behind the wheelchair pushing it. Then, as if watching a movie, she observed Ashley approach Sam. As she had earlier, Ashley formed that same sexy pose in a bikini that left nothing to imagination.

Sam stiffened then made a move to walk away.

Just then, Jess approached them. Sam beamed at Jesse, wrapped an arm around her shoulder, and pulled her close for a quick hug. Even from a distance, Gabby could see the look of shock on Ashley's face. She couldn't hear what was being said, but she saw Ashley's look change to one of anger before she turned and walked away, glancing back once at Sam and Jess.

The scene that had played out in front of her increased Gabby's decision to stay as far away from Ashley as possible. She finished her breakfast and went to her stateroom to get ready for the excursion to Tortola.

Cane Garden Bay on Tortola was the perfect place for snorkeling. Beautiful white sand met turquoise water. On the shore, plenty of drinks and food were available for those who chose not to take part in snorkeling. Gabby was surprised to learn that Tortola was known for growing spices and made a mental note to buy some before heading back to the ship.

Gabby had been snorkeling once before on a trip to Florida. She couldn't wait to see what treasures awaited her beneath the surface of this water. There were eleven people in her group, including Hank, and Tiffany Wainwright, a single, attractive woman from Massachusetts who'd struck up a conversation with Gabby.

They were all fitted to masks and flippers, and then a crew member and a driver took them out in the bay, anchored the boat, and jumped into the water with them.

"Stay fairly close to the boat, so we're here to help you if you need it," counseled the crew member, whose name was Matt. "And remember to keep your T-shirts on, or your backs are going to get burned from the sun. Does everyone have a partner?"

"Can I partner with you and Tiffany?" asked Hank. "I'm the odd man out."

"Sure," said Tiffany.

Hank gave Gabby a questioning look.

She nodded. "Of course. Welcome aboard or something like that."

He laughed. "Thanks."

The group broke apart, heading in different directions.

Hank stayed with Gabby and Tiffany as they swam along the surface of the water.

Beneath them bright-colored fish darted about near the reefs. When a large school of fish turned and headed right for her, Gabby quickly backpaddled, earning a laugh from Hank. She lifted her head out of the water, removed her mouthpiece, and gulped in fresh air.

Hank treaded water nearby, removed his snorkel, and faced her. "Are you all right?"

She grinned. "I was a little scared by the fish being so close to me, but I'm okay. Thanks."

"C'mon, let's get back to it. It's too fantastic to miss."

They put in their mouthpieces and took off side by side to where Tiffany was swimming. She acknowledged them, and they circled the tender and headed in a different direction.

As she became a part of the underwater scene again, Gabby knew she'd never forget the magic of this world. She was swimming along when a hand gripped her ankle and pulled her backward. She knew who it was and allowed Hank to bring her closer.

"We shouldn't get too far from the boat," he said, facing her while treading water.

She followed him to the tender, pleased he was looking out for her.

Later aboard the shuttle back to the ship, Gabby studied the other members of her tour. She loved the idea of meeting people from many different parts of the country. They all seemed as happy as she with the day's events.

Aboard the ship, Gabby said goodbye to everyone and hurried to her stateroom, anxious for a shower and a change of clothes.

As she approached her room, she noticed the cabin

steward, Ricardo, leaving Ashley and Hank's room looking a bit disheveled. He didn't speak as he hurried by her, making her curiosity grow.

Inside the room, she saw a note from Jess to join her, Ellie, and Arabelle in the dining room for afternoon tea. Pleased, she hurried into the shower to wash off the salty substance lingering on her body. She liked the fact that Jess was spending time with Arabelle. Jess's relationship with Sam was moving at a fast pace, but there seemed to be so many things right about it, including being with a very important family member.

Gabby easily found the table and the three other women sitting there in the dining room.

"So glad you could make it," said Ellie. "How was your snorkeling excursion?"

"Fantastic," Gabby said, taking her seat at the table. "Such a beautiful world. I was thrilled to see it."

"Sam and I are going snorkeling later on in the cruise," said Jess.

"The kids wanted to make sure I got to my spa session and special therapy program," said Arabelle. "Sam takes very good care of me." She turned to Jess. "And you are supportive of that."

"Sam has told me about all the things you've done for him," Jess replied quietly. "I'm happy to help."

A waiter came over to them with a three-tiered metal rack holding china plates with an assortment of sandwiches, cakes, scones, and biscuits.

"I've taken the liberty of ordering for everyone," said Ellie.

The waiter offered them cream, lemon, and sugar for their tea. Each woman chose what she wanted. For Gabby, it was simply lemon.

After everyone was settled with their tea and a selection from the food offerings, they sipped and ate quietly for a few moments. Gabby savored this time with women. Having grown up without a mother, it was especially touching to see the friendship between Arabelle and Ellie and their willingness to include Jess and her. Though her father had been a wonderful dad, she'd missed a lot by not having her mother around.

"Thank you for asking me," Gabby said. "I've never been to a formal tea before. My mother died when I was born, and my father never remarried. I'm happy to be here with all of you."

"It's a lovely way to share time with friends," said Ellie. "The cream teas John and I had in London were fabulous. I thought it was a great idea for the four of us to get to know one another better."

"Ellie, no wonder you were such a success with the Sanderling Cove Inn," said Arabelle. "You have a way of making everyone feel comfortable. You've certainly made my cruise very special." She turned to Jess. "What about you, Jess? Gabby told us a little about her. Tell us about your family."

Jess glanced at Gabby before turning back to Arabelle. "I'm one of four girls, the second youngest. We grew up in Ellenton, New York, where Gabby and I met. My parents are still together, now living in Florida, and very much in love. Your typical family, I guess."

"Four girls in the house growing up?" Ellie said. "Your father must be a saint."

Jess laughed. "Selective hearing probably helped him. Mom swears he learned to tune us out the minute we became teenagers."

"You were friends growing up?" Ellie said to Gabby.

"Yes, best friends. We still are," Gabby said. "Jess and my Dad were my family. Now I'm in a big sister program for kids in foster care. I help a little girl named Saree, who was born with Fetal Alcohol Syndrome and needs extra help with things."

"What a sweet idea," said Arabelle. "The two of you young women make my heart sing with how caring you are."

The conversation continued with tidbits of their lives shared easily.

Later, as the four of them got ready to leave, Ellie pulled Gabby aside. "I saw you with your male friend today coming back from the snorkeling excursion. There's something special between the two of you." Ellie beamed at her. "I just know it."

Gabby grinned. "I'm going to tell John on you. He doesn't like you playing matchmaker."

Ellie waved away her concern. "Not to worry. He knows I have an instinct about such things."

Still smiling, Gabby watched Ellie walk away.

"What's going on?" asked Jess.

"Ellie believes there's something special between Hank and me," said Gabby, chuckling.

"Nothing to laugh about," said Jess grinning. "Anyone can see that."

"Enough about Hank and me. You and Sam certainly gave Ashley a surprise this morning. Guess what? Later, I saw our dear cabin steward, Ricardo, leaving Ashley's room, and I don't think he'd just been delivering fresh towels."

Jess wiggled her eyebrows. "She's a piece of work. Sam thinks she's trouble."

"Hank's definitely no longer a fan. Seeing her in action was enough to turn him off. He learned what kind of person she really is and wants no part of her. Poor guy still has to share a stateroom with that woman."

"He can sleep on the couch in our room anytime it becomes too much," said Jess. Her cheeks flushed a bright red. "Sam has asked me to join him in his room one night. I think that might happen." Tears filled her eyes. "I can't believe I've found someone like him. It's as if I've been waiting for him all this time. The more we know about one another, the more perfect it seems."

"Still, you don't want to rush things," Gabby said, studying the way Jess had clasped her hands in a prayerful way.

"He's not pushing me, just wants to let me know he's open to it. If anything, he's more cautious than I am, and I'm not about to make a fool of myself."

Gabby hugged her. "I'm sure things will work out the way they're meant to be. I adore Arabelle. She's a fabulous woman, and she's raised Sam to be a wonderful man."

"I've sent a picture of the two of us together to my

parents. They can't wait to meet him. Of course, I'm the last one to get married, so I'm sure it's a big relief to them that I've found someone I'm serious about after Mark. They never liked Mark. But I'm pretty sure they're going to like Sam. We already have an international flavor to my family with one of my sisters married to an Asian man, another to a Native American."

Gabby grinned. She'd always loved Jess's family.

As Gabby and Jess were about to enter their stateroom, Hank met them at their door. "Are either of you interested in going out to dinner? I can't deal with going to the dining room with Ashley."

"I have an idea," said Jess. "Sam talked about going to the Italian restaurant tonight. He's making reservations. Why don't you and Gabby join us? It'll make a nice foursome."

The relief that spread across Hank's face was almost comical. "That sounds fantastic. Let me know."

"Come on into our room," said Gabby. "Jess can call him from there. I take it things aren't going well with Ashley."

Hank shook his head. "Ashley can put on a convincing pretense, but when you're forced to spend prolonged time with someone, you get to know the real person. It's pretty ugly. After our argument, she told me I was just someone to fill time with until she finds something better. As soon as she gets off the ship back in port, she's meeting up with a guy she dated in college who plays on a baseball team in Florida."

"She's pretty mad at you," said Gabby. She held back on telling Hank about Ricardo. It wasn't her business and might cause more problems.

Jess placed her hands on her hips and shook her head. "Ashley's been outrageous with Sam. I told Gabby you're welcome to sleep on the couch in here if you need to stay away from her."

"Thanks. It might come to that," said Hank. He sighed and studied Gabby. "I have a feeling Dad knew exactly what he was doing when he encouraged me to go on this trip."

"Your father is a shrewd man," said Jess, giving him a knowing look.

"That's why he's been so successful," added Gabby. "Not that he flaunts his success."

"He's very frugal," Hank admitted. "And in this case, he was right about giving me a chance to understand how Ashley really is. Now that I've seen it, I'm done."

"Out of everything bad comes some good," said Jess. "You can hang with us. Let me call Sam and check on tonight."

While Jess made her call, Gabby stepped out onto the balcony. The salty air caressed her cheeks in refreshing strokes. She couldn't hold back a satisfied sigh. It had been a busy, delightful day.

Hank stepped behind her. "Are you having fun on the cruise?"

She turned to him, "I'm so glad I beat you out for this. It's amazing."

He laughed. "I'm glad you won the tickets too."

Jess joined them. "Sam said he has reservations for eight o'clock, and the four of us are set. That gives us time to relax before dinner."

"Sounds perfect," said Gabby.

"Thanks," said Hank. "I'll see you later. Why don't I stop by the room just before eight? I'll walk you to the restaurant."

"Okay," said Gabby, pleased. From the time they first met, she'd thought he was good-looking and nice, but she hadn't let herself think about dating him because she needed to focus on work. Before her father died, he'd encouraged her to try a job at the dealership. Now, seeing how kind and thoughtful Hank was, Gabby wondered about the future. Especially now that they'd no longer be working together.

After Hank left, Jess turned to her. "Gabby Willets, if you don't see the way Hank looks at you, you're crazy. Ellie's right. There's magic there. Relax and enjoy the cruise with him. As the ship's name indicates, Tropical Magic is here for both of us."

Gabby studied her. "Okay, I'm going to do just that for the rest of the cruise. Why not? This was supposed to be a magical time for both of us, right?"

"That's my girl," said Jess. She wiggled her eyebrows playfully. "Remember, a boatload of fun awaits us."

Gabby laughed and hoped Jess was right.

Chapter Six

When Hank stopped by the stateroom before dinner, he carried his suitcase. "Thanks for the offer for me to sleep on the couch. I can't stay in the room with Ashley."

"No problem," said Jess. "But if you are a snorer, you might end up on the balcony."

Hank laughed. "I don't think I'm that bad."

"What happened?" Gabby asked.

"Ashley said she's expecting company and told me to get out. I couldn't pack quickly enough. She's a psycho."

"She's always been able to get her way," said Gabby. "Your ending the relationship must be a shock to her system."

"Watch out," said Hank. "She's upset with you, too."

Gabby shook her head. "I can't worry about that. I'm here to have fun, not fight with someone."

"I'm sorry about all this," said Hank. "It's driving Ashley crazy that her younger sister is getting married soon, and she's not engaged in time for the wedding. That finally came out during one of our arguments."

"Let's go have a nice dinner and forget about that woman," said Jess.

They left the stateroom and headed to the restaurant, which was situated near the theater.

Gabby was excited about the evening. She'd worn the white-eyelet dress she loved and thought it looked especially nice with the suntan she was acquiring. Though he hadn't said a word, she knew from the looks he gave her that Hank liked her dress too.

Sam met them outside the restaurant.

Gabby observed the way his eyes lit up at the sight of Jess. There was no denying the attraction between them.

She turned to Hank and realized that he was staring at her instead of looking at them.

"You look spectacular," he said quietly. "No matter how unpleasant Ashley is making things. I'm glad we're getting to know one another better."

Warmed by the compliment, Gabby returned his smile. "Me too."

They were guided to a table for four inside the restaurant. Gabby took a seat and gazed around the room. If she wasn't aware of the slight movement of the ship at sea, she might think she was in a restaurant in New York. Starched white-linen cloths covered the tables, sconces on the pale-blue walls provided soft lighting, and the aromas emanating from the kitchen were mouthwatering.

A waiter appeared to take their drink orders and give them menus. Sam suggested sharing a bottle of red wine, and Gabby and the others quickly agreed.

After a wine had been selected and served, Gabby turned to Sam. "Thank you for including Hank and me. It's a lovely restaurant, and everything smells and sounds so delicious."

"You're welcome. I'm glad to have this opportunity to get to know you better. Jess talks about you a lot," Sam said, smiling at her. "I thought dinner together was a great idea."

Gabby studied his face and liked the way his eyes met her with a friendly openness. There was an intangible air of kindness about him. She was certain his bedside manner was a huge comfort to any patient of his.

"Jess tells me you practice family medicine," she said. "Why that?"

"At one time, I thought about going into a cardiac practice, but when I realized how many children and families aren't getting adequate health care and how it was tied together, I wanted to help. Health in a family can make a huge difference in how they succeed in society, especially with how addiction is playing a part in so many families. A doctor doesn't treat one member of a family. In many ways, he treats all of them."

"I'm big sister to a little girl who was born with Fetal Alcohol Syndrome. Her mother's addiction ruined her baby's chances for a normal life, but her foster family is doing what they can to help her. Me, too."

"That's very kind of you," said Sam.

Jess interrupted them. "Oh, oh. Don't look now, but Ashley is here with a date. One of the guys I saw her with at the pool."

They were quiet as a hostess guided Ashley and her date past them to a table at a distance away.

Gabby watched them. Even after they moved on, she remained silent, still affected by the glare Ashley had sent her way. Gabby tuned into what Hank was saying about the automobile business.

"Fortunately, I have an excellent product to sell without a lot of unnecessary hoopla." Hank turned to Gabby. "We both do."

"I heard you're leaving the Lexus dealership and going to another one in the next town over from Ellenton," said Jess.

"Yeah, that's going to be a challenge because I'll be competing against the sales force where Gabby will still work."

"And I intend to make sure we win," said Gabby with a teasing grin.

Hank groaned with exaggeration. "That's what I'm afraid of."

They all laughed, but Gabby meant what she said, and Hank knew it.

They were eating peacefully when Ashley approached the table. "What a nice little foursome. I hope you're enjoying your vacation, Gabby. You deserve a little souvenir."

She picked up Gabby's wine glass and tossed the wine onto Gabby's dress. "Oops."

Hank jumped to his feet. "Enough, Ashley. Get lost! Gabby hasn't done anything to you."

A waiter rushed over to them. "Can I help?" He handed a napkin to Gabby and remained at Gabby's side, blocking Ashley.

"Leave now," Hank said to Ashley in a low, threatening voice.

Ashley tried to sashay away, but she stumbled and almost fell.

"Oh, look! She's drunk," hissed Jess.

"Are you all right, Gabby?" Hank asked, looking and sounding distressed.

"I will be, but my dress probably won't," she answered, feeling the sting of tears.

"That little bitch," murmured Jess, getting to her feet. "C'mon, I'll go to the ladies' room with you to help you get it cleaned up."

"There is a dry-cleaning service aboard the ship," offered the waiter. "But wine is pretty hard to get off."

Gabby stood. "I won't be gone long. I think it's a lost cause."

Inside the ladies' room, Jess helped her remove what wine they could off the dress.

"I'm so sorry, Gabby. I know you were so excited about finding this dress on sale. It's just like Ashley to do something so spiteful."

"Hank is right. Ashley is out of control. And if she has a drinking problem, I just want to stay out of her way. I remember a time from high school when she did a similar thing to a girl her boyfriend dated after he dumped her."

Jess took hold of Gabby's arm and gave her a look of concern. "Let's not allow this to ruin our evening. It's been enjoyable getting to know Hank, and I noticed you and Sam talking. That means so much to me."

"You're right," Gabby responded, willing her anger away. "We can't let this spoil the night. After dinner, I'll go up to the stateroom and change my clothes."

"Thanks," said Jess. "I love you, girl."

"Love you too. Now let's get back to our dinner."

Gabby and Jess rejoined the men at the table, and after feeling a little awkward about the big stain down the front of her dress, Gabby settled in for a delightful dinner.

After changing her dress in her stateroom, Gabby joined Jess, Sam, and Hank on the Lido deck. It was another starry evening, and the four of them were still enjoying one another's company.

At one point, Sam and Hank left to check out one of the game rooms, leaving Jess and Gabby alone to talk.

"I like Sam," said Gabby. "He's a very nice man, and I'm sure a fantastic doctor."

"He's pretty exceptional," said Jess. "We'll see what the future brings. I just hope this isn't a cruise-ship-romance thing. I don't think so because we both feel so strongly about one another."

"Sam doesn't seem like the kind of man who would participate in something like that," said Gabby. "Especially after introducing you to Arabelle." She shook her head and sighed. "I have to admit this cruise has turned out to be something totally different from what I thought."

"Aren't you still glad you won the winning tickets?" Jess said, smiling.

"Oh, yes," Gabby said truthfully, but she, like Jess, wondered what things would be like once the cruise was over.

Later, when Gabby announced that she was going to bed, Hank said, "I'll walk you to the room."

Jess and Sam exchanged long looks; then Jess said, "I'll meet up with you two later."

Sam put his arm around Jess. "We're going to enjoy some alone time. My grandmother won't need me until tomorrow morning. I checked on her before dinner."

Gabby waved goodbye and left with Hank.

"Hope it's not going to be too awkward with me staying in the room with the two of you," said Hank to Gabby.

"It shouldn't be." She liked that he was making his position clear. It saved them both a lot of trouble because as much as she liked him, she was not going to be a rebound for him.

When they reached the stateroom, Hank said, "I'll wait outside here while you change clothes, if you like."

"No need," she said. "I'll change in the bathroom." He'd seen her in her bikini plenty of times wearing less than what she wore to bed—sleep shorts and a T-shirt.

When she opened the bathroom door after changing, she noticed Hank wearing swim trunks and realized they would be very civilized about sharing a room.

Gabby found sheets and a light blanket on a shelf in the closet and helped him make up the pull-out couch. "Looks pretty comfy," she said.

Hank gave her a rueful look. "I won't have to fall asleep wondering if I'm going to be stabbed in the night."

"It's such a shame that things have gone so badly for you," said Gabby. "I didn't know Ashley had a problem with alcohol."

"I was beginning to doubt the relationship even before we got on the ship," confessed Hank. "But I chalked her behavior up to us both being stressed about making last-minute arrangements. The truth is, I was dating Ashley but not spending quality time with her. That's something I won't do again."

"We all make mistakes," said Gabby remembering the man she'd dated in New York. He also had problems that hadn't shown up right away.

"Well, goodnight," said Hank. "See you in the morning." He turned out the light on the end table and stretched out on the bed.

Not knowing when Jess would return, Gabby did the same. A soft glow from the full moon shining on the water outside gave her the ability to see Hank lying on his back, staring up at the ceiling.

"Tell me more about your life before moving to Ellenton," she said, curious about him. "You told me you worked for your stepfather's friend. When did you decide to help your dad?"

"My job with my stepfather's friend required long hours and was very regimented. Though I wanted to please my stepfather, I was relieved when my own dad reached out to me. Since I've worked at the dealership with him, I've grown to love and respect my father deeply. He's a decent man."

"My father respected him too," said Gabby. "He's the one who suggested I go to work at the dealership. He was aware that not only did I know about cars, but I needed to get out and meet people."

"You obviously are well-suited for the job," said Hank in a begrudging manner that made them both laugh. "I'm glad you got to make this trip, though. You haven't traveled much?"

"No," said Gabby. "While I was growing up, we couldn't afford it. Then I was living in New York, which is expensive. So, Jess and I took short trips here and there, but nothing too fancy."

"I've been lucky. My mother and stepfather took me lots of places when I was young. Later, on my own, I traveled all over Europe. That was a great experience. I hope you get to do that one day."

"Me, too. I'd also like to take another cruise," she said.

"One without Ashley aboard?" Hank said, teasing her.

She laughed. "You got it."

They lay quietly for a while, and then soft snores came from across the room. Gabby shut her eyes and went to sleep, wondering if this was how it would be for the rest of the cruise.

Chapter Seven

Gabby awoke with a start and realized Jess wasn't in her bed, and Hank was still asleep on the couch. Bleary-eyed, she got up and then noticed Jess on the balcony. After taking care of her morning routines, she joined Jess outside.

"What are you doing out here?" said Gabby quietly. "It's a little chilly."

Jess wrapped a blanket tighter around herself. "It feels nice. Very refreshing."

"What time did you get in? I didn't hear you."

Jess shook her head. "You couldn't, with Hank snoring. But he soon stopped. Sam and I stayed up until two o'clock talking. We know there are challenges ahead, but we both want to see where this could go. Not only is the chemistry between us stinkin' hot, we really like one another. We've been honest about it. Things could change once we get off the ship and back to our usual lives. Especially for Sam and his heavy workload." She gave Gabby a glum look.

Gabby studied her troubled face. "Why don't you do what you tell me and simply enjoy the cruise. The rest will come later."

"I never expected this to happen," said Jess, "but you're right. I can't let it ruin my vacation with you. Let's go have breakfast and hope Ellie and John are there. I need to talk to her."

"Okay. But we can't leave Hank here asleep, can we?"

"Why not? The poor guy probably hasn't had a decent sleep since he's come aboard," said Jess.

They went inside and were tiptoeing across the room when Hank stirred. He sat up on one elbow and scowled. "What are you two up to?"

"We're going to breakfast. But you can stay in bed. We'll be as quiet as we can," said Gabby, taking in every detail of his very masculine body.

He flopped back down on the pillow. "See you later."

They dressed and left the room as quickly and quietly as possible.

⚓

When they approached their table in the dining room, Ellie and John were already seated.

"Oh, Ellie," gushed Jess. "I'm so glad to see you. I need some advice."

"About Sam?" Ellie asked, beaming.

John rolled his eyes.

Gabby laughed and took a seat beside Jess. She could hardly wait to tell John about the food at the Italian restaurant. Ellie had mentioned they were saving that meal for one of the last evenings of the cruise.

While Gabby and John talked, Jess and Ellie conversed quietly. Gabby was glad for the friendship that had developed between them. She realized it was easy for some people quickly to become close on cruises.

"You're going to be fine, Jessica," said Ellie as Gabby tuned into their conversation. "You and Sam are approaching this attraction wisely. His grandmother is a lovely person, and so is he. It's a matter of letting things evolve as they will." Her eyes twinkled. "But I know everything will turn out right. I just do."

Jess and Gabby exchanged glances, and then Jess said, "Me, too. Thanks for saying that. I needed to hear it."

"Anytime," said Ellie giving her a triumphant smile that brought a soft groan from John.

"She's an incurable optimist," he said.

"Yes, I am," said Ellie. "Now, Gabby, how are you and your young man doing?"

Gabby's eyes widened. "Are you talking about Hank and me?"

"Yes, I am," Ellie said.

"Wait until you hear this," said Jess, leaning forward to tell the story of the incident in the restaurant.

"What kind of wine was it?" John asked, bringing a laugh from each of them.

After breakfast, Gabby and Jess signed up for the submarine excursion in Barbados. Something Ellie recommended. When they discovered the excursion was wheelchair accessible, Jess called Sam to tell him. Gabby phoned Hank and asked if he wanted her to sign him up.

"I'll be right there," Hank said.

He met them, along with Sam, who signed up his grandmother and himself for it.

Pleased it would be a congenial group, Gabby and Jess went back to the stateroom to change from bathing suits to different, more comfortable clothes.

After the tour, they were all going to have lunch at one of the restaurants in Bridgetown, maybe tour the Mount Gay Rum Visitor Center, or do some shopping.

Aboard the submarine, Gabby found a place to perch by one of the windows and stared out at the scene. Fish swam by, and Gabby remembered how fantastic it had been actually to swim with them. Her favorite part of the tour was when they went deeper to see a ship-wreck. Life below the water was both exciting and dangerous. Reefs could destroy boats even as they protected land.

She glanced at Hank and recalled his enthusiasm for snorkeling and liked how he was enjoying this. She real-ized that though they'd worked together for a little over a year, she hadn't known him at all.

"What do you think?" he asked her. "Seeing the wreck reminds me of favorite pirate movies. I know real pirates didn't live a glamorous life, but it was an adventure all the same for a boy growing up in the desert."

"I never wanted to be on a pirate ship. But a trip to outer space? I always loved that idea," Gabby replied.

"I like that idea myself." Hank grinned at her. "Who knows? It might happen for all of us sooner than we think."

After the tour was over, they all agreed to have lunch at a restaurant along the beach. They asked a driver for a recommendation, and he took them to a place down the coast where a beautiful restaurant provided outdoor seating on a wooden deck.

A hostess accepted their request for seats on the deck. Crisp, white-linen cloths covered the tables that had been pushed together to accommodate their group of seven. They had an uninterrupted view of the lush, turquoise waters of the Caribbean Sea.

Gazing out at the water, Gabby felt the gentle breeze in her hair and let out a long sigh of satisfaction. She knew how lucky she was to be there, but suddenly Gabby wished her father could see this. He'd never had the chance to do something like this, and she missed him.

A waiter came to take their drink orders and to hand out menus. One look at the menu and Gabby sighed happily again. She turned to John. "The selection looks terrific."

"Yes, it does," said John. "I'm going to order anything I want." He shot Ellie a defiant look that amused Gabby. "I'm going for the Chicken and Mushroom Linguine with a creamy chardonnay sauce."

Ellie gave him a worried look, but she didn't say

anything. Ellie had told them that John had had a heart attack a couple of years ago, and she fussed over him about it.

"And how about you?" John asked Gabby.

"Simple, I'm going for Bajan Fried Flying Fish with the Caper Dressing and a mixed green salad with a lime vinaigrette." Gabby loved trying something new. Though they didn't have a lot of money when she was growing up, her father liked to cook and introduced her to a variety of food.

As they all chatted and ate together, Gabby observed the way Jess and Sam were talking and laughing. From across the table, Ellie winked at her, and Gabby knew she too was feeling as if those two belonged together.

The next day, after a whale-watching excursion off of Dominica, Gabby couldn't wait to get into her swimsuit and take a dip in the pool. She still wasn't used to the warmth and humidity of such a tropical climate. Hank politely waited for her to get changed before he took over the room.

As Gabby waited for Hank in the hallway, she saw a steward carry out suitcases from the stateroom next door.

"Where are you going with that luggage?" Gabby asked. "They belong to an acquaintance of mine."

"She's getting off the ship. Medical reasons," the steward said. "You'll have to get any information directly from her."

Just as Gabby lifted her cell to call Jess, it rang. *Jess.*

"You won't guess what happened," Jess said without even bothering to say hello. "The latest news is that Ashley has a severe sunburn, fainted because she was so dehydrated, and broke her wrist. She's being taken to the Princess Margaret Hospital in Roseau. She told the doctors she doesn't want to return to the ship; she wants to go home no matter what."

"Was Sam able to see her?"

"He's at the infirmary now. As much as Ashley has hurt me in the past, I would never want something like this to happen to her," said Jess.

"Me, either," said Gabby, shocked by the turn of events.

"Earlier, I'd overheard Sam warn Ashley about getting too much sun, but she laughed it off," said Jess. "She must be way sorry now."

"It's hard to troll when you're all covered up," Gabby said, unable to hold back her sarcasm. She'd watched Ashley in action. Her posing had sent a very blatant message.

"I'll tell Hank what happened," Gabby told Jess. "I'm sure he'll want to speak to her."

Gabby knocked on the door to the stateroom.

Hank opened it, wearing swim trunks. "Ready to go?"

"I've got some news for you about Ashley," she began.

He frowned. "What did she do now?"

"She's hurt and is being taken to the hospital in Roseau."

"What happened?" Shock whitened his complexion.

Gabby gave him all the details. "I thought you might

want to go to the infirmary to see her before they take her ashore."

"Definitely," said Hank. "Want to come with me?"

"Actually, I do," Gabby said. "I'm sorry this has happened to her."

"Me, too," said Hank. "This whole cruise has been a disaster for her."

⚓

The infirmary was located in one of the lower decks of the ship and looked pretty typical with a couple of hospital beds, an examination area, and plenty of supplies.

Sam and Jess were there, but Ashley had already been moved.

"Ashley told me to tell you she's sorry," Jess told Hank.

"What happened? How did she get so burned?" he asked her.

Jess turned to Sam.

"She had too much to drink and fell asleep in the sun without putting sunscreen on her back. Even before today, she was getting too much sun. I tried to warn her to be careful, but she didn't listen. And then it was too late. She was dehydrated and disoriented, and she tripped and fell. She's better off at the hospital, where they will continue to give her fluids and care for the burns. They've wrapped her wrist, but they'll want to get a better look at it and set it properly."

"There's no point in her coming back aboard the ship

for the last few days. She didn't even want to try." Jess shook her head. "She looked awful."

"I'd better go to her," said Hank. "I'm responsible for seeing that she gets home."

"If you hurry, you might be able to catch up to them at the ramp," said Sam. "I'll call Dr. Hubbard and tell him you're on your way." He punched in a number and spoke, then turned to Hank.

"Go ahead and meet them by the ramp. They're ready to take her into Roseau."

Hank gave Gabby a questioning look, and she shook her head. She didn't want to witness that moment.

After Hank left, Jess said, "Guess I'll go up and get changed into a bathing suit. I'm ready for a swim."

"I'll save you a chair," said Gabby. "Please bring my hat." She was usually careful about protecting herself from the sun, but she'd be even more attentive now.

Later, Gabby saw Hank by the pool and waved him over. "How did it go with Ashley? It's such a terrible way for her to end this trip."

Hank plunked down on the empty chair beside her and sighed. "She looked awful. She was stretched out on her stomach on a gurney because it was too painful to sit up. She told me she was sorry, that she screwed up big time."

"It's too bad it happened this way," Gabby said, moving aside so Jess could sit beside her on the chair.

"I'm not sorry the relationship has ended," said Hank. "Still, this is an awful way for the cruise to end for her."

"Ashley sure made it easy for you to break up with her," quipped Jess.

Hank glanced at Gabby and looked away.

Sam joined them.

Jess stood to give him a quick hug.

"Glad to see you're wearing a cover-up," he said to her. "People come aboard the ship, get caught up in the partying, and do crazy things. It's never fun to see."

Hank got to his feet. "I'm going to have a swim. Then I'll go move my stuff back to my room."

After he and Sam went to get into the pool, Jess turned to Gabby. "Now that things have changed with Ashley gone, maybe there's a chance for you to get to know Hank a lot better."

Gabby noted Jess's teasing smile and shook her head. It was crazy to think of anything happening so soon between Hank and her. Right now, the friendship between them seemed awesome.

Chapter Eight

Two days later at breakfast, Ellie said, "I'm inviting you two to join John, Arabelle, Sam, and me for dinner. Hank, too, if you'll be so kind as to invite him. We thought it would be fun to share another meal. The cruise will soon be over, and we won't have many chances to do so."

"That sounds nice," said Gabby. "We all enjoy one another."

"Yes, indeed," said Ellie, smiling. She became serious. "It's such a shame about your friend from New York. I was there when they took her to the infirmary. Very scary."

"We're sorry she went through such an experience," said Gabby.

"Ashley is obnoxious and sometimes mean, but something like that shouldn't happen to anybody," Jess said.

"It was very kind of Hank to pick up the expense of flying her home," said Ellie, "but then he's a very nice young man."

As Ellie's gaze settled on her, Gabby nodded her agreement. She was discovering what a gentleman Hank was. Twice, when Jess and Sam needed some quiet moments together, Hank had allowed Gabby to spend some time in his room. Though they were both attracted to one another, they had yet to act on it. It was the responsible way to act.

At least that's what she told herself.

That evening, they gathered together in the dining room, a comfortable group. The earlier excursion into the rainforest on St. Lucia, taking a mud bath, soaking in mineral baths, and refreshing herself in waterfalls had left her feeling depleted of energy. But a brief nap before dinner had Gabby reenergized, and she was delighted to be included in the group.

Sitting next to Arabelle, Gabby listened to her tell some stories of politics in New York. Like every other state, it had its own bad and good players. Arabelle's husband was one of the best guys, and was still respected after his death several years ago.

Gabby observed the interaction between Arabelle and Jess and was happy to see that Jess, as usual, had earned a new friend. But then, Jess's energy, laugh, and tenderness were all things Gabby already knew about her.

From the looks he kept giving Jess, Sam knew all about those qualities and more. Their quick romance had been such a surprise but a good one. Jess might be friendly, but she didn't usually give her heart away quickly or to just anyone.

Hank caught her smiling at them and winked at her.

She let out a soft chuckle. She was pretty sure he was interested in a relationship with her that was more than friendship.

When dinner was over, Ellie and Arabelle announced they were going to the show. John said he would try his luck in the casino, leaving the two couples to make plans of their own.

"How about the four of us going up to listen to the music on the Lido deck?" said Jess.

"I'll go for a while," Gabby said, "but then I'm going to bed. I haven't signed up for an excursion per se in Antigua for tomorrow, but Hank and I thought it might be interesting to tour St. John's and sample some native dishes."

"Jess and I have already talked about it. We're going to stay aboard the ship and keep my grandmother company," said Sam.

The grins Sam and Jess exchanged made Gabby think they would do something more than that.

"C'mon," said Hank. "Before you go to bed, I want at least one dance with you."

The four of them went to the Lido deck and found seats at one of the bars.

Gabby ordered a club soda with a squeeze of lime and sat back, more relaxed than she'd been since forever. She knew she'd be busy once she was back home, but tonight and the last couple of days of the cruise, she intended simply to enjoy herself.

She noticed others in the crowd must have decided to do the same thing because the loud, raucous noise of people celebrating the first days of the cruise had softened into something less frantic.

"May I have this dance?" Hank asked her with a small bow.

"Yes, please," said Gabby, playing along by giving him a curtsey before walking out onto the dance floor.

Romantic music swirled around them as they began to sway. Gabby closed her eyes and rested her head against Hank's broad chest. Being in his arms felt so right. She knew she'd never be able to work with him again without remembering this moment. She gazed up at him and saw from the look he gave her that he was feeling this special moment too.

When the song ended, they pulled apart and stared at one another, sending silent messages to each other.

"Why don't we go to my room? We'll have privacy there," Hank suggested, wrapping an arm around her.

"Okay." Gabby's pulse raced. She studied him a moment, wondering if she was right to take this step with him. There'd be no turning back to a time when they could pretend that they weren't attracted to one another. It was a risk. At least if things didn't work out between them, she wouldn't have the problem of working with him. He'd be gone to his new job.

He gave her a questioning look. Gabby took hold of his hand. Only then did she notice that Sam and Jess had already left.

⚓

Standing outside his stateroom door, Gabby wondered again if they were rushing things. True, they'd talked for hours and hours, had spent time together doing all kinds of activities, but they hadn't even kissed beyond an earlier kiss on the lips. That was the trouble. That kiss had sent heat roaring through her body, filling her with need.

"Are you sure about this?" Hank asked. His bright-blue gaze assessed her.

Gabby drew in a deep breath and nodded. If she were totally honest with herself, she'd been attracted to him for months. But now that she'd had time to get to know him in a whole different way, those feelings were becoming deeper, more real.

Inside the stateroom, Hank opened the sliding door to the balcony, stepped outside, and turned to her. "Beautiful moon tonight. Come share it with me before we go back inside."

She walked toward him, basking in his smile. She realized he was as nervous as she and loved him for it.

He put an arm around her, and they stood looking at the night sky. The light from the moon made a glowing trail across the moving water. Gabby whimsically wondered what might be at the far end of it.

Hank turned her face toward him, caressed her with his gaze, then lowered his lips to hers. His kiss was warm, sure, and tender. A soft whimper escaped her.

He rubbed her back and pulled her closer as if to protect her, but it only added to her pulsing need.

When they finally pulled apart, they simply stared at one another.

"I knew it could be like that with you," he murmured. "But, wow!"

She grinned. "I had no idea ..."

As he led her inside, Gabby could hardly wait to experience more of the emotions whirling inside her.

Later, Gabby discovered what she'd been missing all along when Hank showed her what it was like to be truly loved. Knowing Jess and Sam were in the stateroom next door, Gabby happily settled in Hank's bed for the night.

Gabby stirred in her sleep and became aware of a form next to her. Then it all came back. Last night wasn't a sensual dream but as real as the man beside her. She gazed at Hank, lying on his back sleeping peacefully. She reached out, touching him lightly on the cheek as if to prove he was there.

He opened his eyes sleepily, and then a wide smile crossed his face at the sight of her. "Hey, good morning."

"Good morning to you," she said, happiness flooding her when he drew her closer.

"What are we going to do today? Do you want to get off the ship or stay on board?" He asked, rubbing her back.

He propped himself up on one elbow. "We'd talked about going ashore and tasting some native food. Do you still want to do that?"

"I think I'd rather stay on board. There's plenty of tasty food here, and I want to have some more time alone with you," she said. "Would you mind if we didn't leave the ship?"

"Staying onboard sounds great," he said. "I was hoping you'd say that."

"We have only a couple of days before we go home and get back into our competition," Gabby said.

He gave her a teasing grin. "Competition, huh? You're not going to let that go?"

"Absolutely not," she said with resolve, and they both laughed.

"Seriously, the fact that I'll be working at a different dealership should make things easier for us to date. Dad can't say or do anything about our breaking the rules he has set in place."

"Do you think Ashley is going to be a problem? She's made a big mistake," said Gabby. The Ashley she knew wouldn't let this cruise stop her from trying to make up with Hank or creating trouble for them.

"No, if she tries, I'll take care of it," Hank replied. "She really fooled me."

She gazed at his rueful expression. "We all make mistakes. Believe me, I've made a few myself, dating men who weren't right for me. It's easy to get trapped in a relationship when the other person makes it effortless just to keep going. Let's make a pact to be totally honest with each other."

"Agreed," he said. "I'm being totally honest with you when I say I'm falling in love with you. I think it started the first day we met. But I couldn't acknowledge it."

"That makes me so happy," said Gabby. "I feel the same way."

Later, while Hank showered, Gabby went next door to her room. She found it empty of people, but a note from Jess was taped to the desk that said she and Sam were going onshore.

The phone rang. Gabby picked it up. "Hi, I thought I'd go down and grab us some breakfast and bring it back to your room," said Hank. "Sound okay?"

"More than okay, fantastic. And make my coffee black, please."

They hung up, and Gabby went into the shower, pleased to have this time alone.

As Gabby toweled herself off, she stared at the image in the mirror and saw a new brightness to her features. Her brown eyes sparkled, and a smile played at the corner of her lips. Though her relationship with Hank was new, a feeling of rightness about it seemed as old as time. Even though she had more to learn about him, they fit together in so many ways.

Hank arrived wearing bathing trunks and flip-flops and carrying a tray with two cups of coffee and a variety of breakfast items. He set it down on top of the desk in the room. "Breakfast awaits you, mademoiselle."

"Wonderful," she said, picking up a cup of coffee and taking a satisfying sip of it.

"Where are Jess and Sam?" asked Hank.

Gabby showed him the note.

Hank grinned. "Your place or mine?"

Gabby laughed. "Let's give the staff time to clean the

rooms while we go down to the pool. I'd like to do a few laps in it."

"Okay, then maybe I can get you to try the water slide," he said, elbowing her. "I heard you tell Jess you didn't think you could do it."

"I still don't think I can. I'm afraid of heights, and even looking at the slide sends goose pimples up and down my back. But I'll cheer you on if you go." The slide extended beyond the side of the ship and had translucent sections that Gabby wasn't sure she could handle, even if she closed her eyes.

"The slide is fun," said Hank, "but I won't push you."

"I don't do well at amusement parks," Gabby confessed. "I get sick on most of the spinning or roller coaster rides."

"What about the race track?" Hank asked. "Will you do that with me?"

"Yes, I think I can do that," Gabby said with more confidence than she felt. "But watch out! I'm pretty good at driving race cars."

"Okay, the challenge is on. Not only are you trying to beat me selling cars, now you want to beat me on the racetrack?" He flexed his muscles and pretended to be driving a car. "You don't know who you're up against, lady."

She sent him a smug look. "We'll see. Let's get to it. I'll take my swim afterward."

Gabby's bravado began to fade a bit when she realized the Go-Kart track sat at the very top of the ship.

Relax, she told herself. *You're a top-notch driver.* She'd participated in some car races a few years ago when she was dating a young man who was all about racing. Before that, she'd spent hours at a nearby race track with her father. He helped maintain some of the cars. She'd learned about that too.

When they arrived at the track, carts were lined up with helmets attached to the steering wheels.

The staff member in charge talked to them about being careful, going only as fast as they were comfortable, and showed them the buttons on the wheel. One said reverse; the other said boost.

"Do not get the buttons mixed up," he joked, and Gabby told herself once more to relax, trying not to glance at the water far below them.

"Ready?" said Hank.

"You bet," Gabby said with a false sense of confidence. She put on her helmet and helped a staff member roll her car to the start line.

While she waited for Hank to get his car in position, she sat behind the wheel trying to get a feel for the cart.

"We'll do a slow run through the course before we start the race," said Hank. "Okay with you?"

Gabby gave him a thumbs up, wishing she could pretend she was on the ground, not on the higher regions of a ship.

They started.

Gabby reveled in the rush of adrenaline that filled her. She was her father's daughter when it came to cars and competition. She hoped that would help her concentrate on the track and not the area around it.

They returned to the start line. The staff member lowered his checkered flag indicating the race had begun.

Gabby took off with a roar. Hank was ahead of her. She gave the engine a boost and scooted around him. From then on, all Gabby saw was the racetrack in front of her, the way the curves seemed to come quicker and quicker. When she crossed the finish line, a bubble of laughter rose out of her for the pure fun of it.

Only then was she aware of Hank in his cart beside her. He took off his helmet and grinned. "Where did you learn to drive like that?"

"My father," she said and felt an unexpected sting of tears. While she'd been busy taking care of him and afterward, taking care of details following his death, she hadn't had much time to face the loss of her father. Grief hit her like a punch to the gut. She took off her helmet and lowered her head on the steering wheel. Sobs rose from within her.

Hank rushed over to her. "Gabby, honey, what's wrong?"

She lifted her tear-streaked face. "I miss my dad."

He helped her out of the cart and into his arms. "I'm sorry. I met him a few times, but he was a great guy. He died much too young. C'mon, let's go somewhere where we can talk."

"I need to get suntan lotion and a coverup to go swimming."

Giving her a look of concern, Hank said, "Okay, but if you want to talk, I'm here."

"Thanks. I need to do that." After saying the words, Gabby realized how true they were. She felt safe with Hank, and rather than stuff her feelings as she usually did, she wanted to talk about her father. The race had brought all her sadness to the surface.

Hank slid his arm around her waist, and they headed to her stateroom. Gabby remembered how conflicted she'd felt as she was about to enter Hank's stateroom last night. But now, as she did then, she felt how right it was to be with him. They still had things to learn about each other, but she knew without a doubt that he was the man she'd been waiting for all her life. She was glad her father had met Hank. That made her fast-growing relationship with Hank seem even better.

Inside the cabin, Hank opened the sliding door to the balcony. "Do you want to sit out here?"

"Yes, that would be perfect." The fresh air and sunshine would be a healthy way to counteract the sorrow that would always be a part of her. "How about a Coke?" Gabby asked him. "I have some in the mini-bar."

"Thanks." Hank waited for her to hand him the drink and then stood aside as she walked out to the balcony and took a seat in a chair close to the door. The views from the balcony were spectacular, but she liked the security of being able to quickly step inside when the distance from the water below began to play with her mind.

"Tell me about your dad," said Hank, sitting in a chair beside her and giving her a look of concern. "I know he was the top mechanic working for my father and that Dad thought very highly of him. He told me they were friends. It's odd, in a way, that with our fathers being friends and working together for so many years, we never really knew one another."

"Maybe that's all part of a plan," said Gabby.

"A plan? Do you think we were meant to meet and ...'? His blue-eyed gaze met her dark eyes and reached inside her.

"And fall in love?" she said softly.

"Yes." Hank smiled, reached over, and tucked a strand of hair behind her ear. Then he kissed her.

When they pulled apart, Gabby let out a sigh. "I know my father would be happy with the idea of my being with you. He admired your dad so much. You're a lot like him, you know."

Hank gave her a pleased look. "Really? I like that. What happened that your father raised you alone?"

"My mother died giving birth to me. It was a tragedy that should never have happened," said Gabby. "But Dad took on the role of both mother and father to me with a lot of affection and determination to do an excellent job. An aunt, my mother's sister, came to live with us for a summer when I was thirteen. That's a difficult age for any girl, especially one without a mother. She helped me with some personal issues and gave me fresh ideas about what I wanted to do in the future. At the end of the summer, she had to return to her job as a school teacher. Both my father and I were relieved when she left, though she and I remain close to this day."

"That's nice," said Hank, studying her and then gazing out at the sea. "Looking back, I probably should have insisted I be given the option of living with my dad, but he and my mother agreed I should stay with her because of his time commitment to his business. I've never been happier than now, living in New York and working with my father. It means a lot to me that he trusts me with his business and will allow me to run it one day."

"It must be a huge relief to him to have you interested in it," said Gabby.

"I think it is. But let's talk about you and your father. You mentioned racing cars reminded you of him," prompted Hank.

"The summer after my aunt left, Dad and I got into racing cars. Well, he did some racing and helped mechanics with cars, but I got to practice driving cars even before I was legally able to do so. It was a secret thrill for both of us."

"That's very cool," said Hank. "Did you ever consider going into racing professionally?"

Gabby chuckled and shook her head. "I dated a driver once, and that was enough to tell me I didn't want that life."

They stared out at the sea. Gabby's thoughts were full of happy years with her father. Then their conversation moved to the devastating moment he was told about his cancer and that he could expect to live for less than a year. That had been one of the worst times of her life.

She felt Hank's arm on her shoulder and realized tears were streaming down her cheeks. He tugged on her hand, and she rose and settled on the lap he offered her. Gabby curled up against his broad chest and let her tears flow, feeling safe in his arms.

Hank rubbed her back in comforting circles.

She lifted her face, unashamed of her wet cheeks. "Thank you, Hank. I haven't been able to do that, and as sad as I feel, I know allowing myself to grieve is healthy for me."

"You were so lucky to have him," Hank said softly. "And he was very, very fortunate to have you in his life."

She stared out at the water, knowing her father's spirit would remain with her forever. She believed things happened for a reason and wondered if he somehow knew it had brought her to this moment with Hank.

Chapter Nine

After sharing her grief with Hank, Gabby felt a new connection to him. He'd been gentle, kind, and thoughtful—all important traits for her in a person. As she told Jess later that day when they were stretched out by the pool, he was the kind of man she'd always dreamed of marrying.

"Marrying? Are you telling me that you and Hank have talked about that? So soon?" Jess said, sitting up and gaping at her.

"Heavens, no, but we are doing a lot of talking and learning about each other. And, I must say, the chemistry is out of sight. He's ... marvelous." Gabby's cheeks were burning, but she couldn't help it. Just thinking of their lovemaking sent a burst of warmth through her body, from the tips of her toes to the top of her head.

"It's the first time I've ever seen you like this," Jess said, smiling at her. "It makes me happy. It's so fabulous that you earned the winning tickets for this trip. Sam and I have decided to keep on seeing one another after the cruise ends. His grandmother is aware and approves. I appreciate that Sam has so much respect and devotion to her."

"I like Sam. The way you two look at each other is enough to create a fire."

"Well, yeah, he's really hot," said Jess. "Who'd a thunk it, huh?"

Gabby and Jess shared a quiet laugh. The cruise was so much more than either had dreamed.

That evening, Jess and Sam had dinner with Arabelle, while Gabby and Hank dined with Ellie and John for a sort-of farewell meal. The next day they would be in St. Thomas, and then they were heading home.

Sitting across the table from her, Gabby thought Ellie looked terrific—tanned and relaxed. John looked as relaxed, though he hadn't spent much time sitting around the pool. Even now, Hank and John were discussing the racetrack and how much fun they were having with it.

Hank put an arm around her. "You should see Gabby on a Go-Kart. She beat me. But then, she's somewhat of a pro."

"Really?" said Ellie, beaming at her.

"My dad used to help at a racetrack doing mechanical work on the cars, and he sometimes raced. That's where I learned to drive. When I was a little older, I competed in races against other women. It was a blast, but I knew I wanted to do that for only a short time."

"Your father sounds like a very nice man and a fun dad," said Ellie.

Gabby smiled. "He was both. Thanks."

Hank squeezed her shoulder, and she glanced at him, grateful for his support.

John offered to select and pay for a bottle of wine, and Gabby and Hank eagerly agreed. She loved listening to John talk about different wines and liked having the opportunity to taste some new ones to her.

After ordering the wine—a French Gamay—John spoke about white wines he and Ellie had tasted in Switzerland. "I've never seen them available in the states. There's an understandable reason why. They're too delicious to export."

Their wine came, and after the process of tasting and approving it, John lifted his glass. "Here's to meeting you and having a wonderful cruise."

They all clinked glasses together.

"I'm so glad you two have made a connection. I tried to tell Gabby earlier ..." Ellie stopped when John elbowed her.

"Ellie and her friends like to play matchmaker," John said.

"And we've had success doing it," Ellie reminded him.

Gabby and Hank looked at each other and chuckled.

"See? I knew it," said Ellie. "You two are perfect together."

Hank lifted his glass. "I'd like to dedicate this next toast to you, Ellie. Keep on doing whatever it is you do."

He winked at Gabby, and she let out a soft giggle of amusement.

Their waiter approached, and they listened to him tell them about the specials of the day. After much indecision, Gabby chose sea bass with a light cream and ginger sauce. Everyone else chose a fish dish, so John ordered another bottle of the Gamay.

"You two will have to come visit us at the Sanderling Cove Inn," said Ellie. "It's a beautiful spot on the Gulf Coast of Florida, a perfect spot for a wedding."

"Ellie, stop," John growled softly.

"Sorry, but two of my granddaughters got married there, and both were gorgeous events," said Ellie. "But enough about that. Will you go back to working together?"

Hank shook his head. "Not really. I'll be moving to another dealership in the next town. So, we won't be in direct competition per se. But my father already believes that one dealership should compete against the other. We'll see."

"It makes it sort of fun when we do compete," said Gabby. "I like winning." She gave Hank a teasing smile that made him burst into laughter.

"Are you two going ashore in St. Thomas?" Ellie asked.

Gabby glanced at Hank and turned to her. "Yes. I want to do some shopping there."

"Me, too," said Ellie. "They have such a variety of things. I thought I'd do some early Christmas shopping. It makes traveling extra fun when I can do that."

Their dinner came, and they grew quiet as they dug

into their meal. One of the things that surprised Gabby was how delicious the food was in the dining room. The buffet served good food too, but Gabby preferred the intimacy of the dining room.

After dinner, Gabby thanked Ellie and John for sharing a lovely meal with them. "I certainly want to keep in touch. If I don't see you for breakfast in the morning or in St. Thomas or anywhere else, maybe I'll make it to Florida some time."

"I hope you do," said Ellie. "Remember what I said about the Sanderling Cove Inn. I'd love to see you there."

Gabby held in a laugh when Ellie winked at her. She was irrepressible.

"Ready to meet Jess and Sam?" Hank asked after Ellie and John hugged them before departing.

"Yes. Jess told me they are planning on seeing each other after the cruise is over. Arabelle likes Jess. I think they're a perfect match."

"Like Ellie thinks of us?" Hank said, laughing and shaking his head. "She's something else."

"It's obvious that John adores her," said Gabby. She liked the idea that Ellie thought she and Hank were perfect together.

Later, sitting with Hank, Jess, and Sam, Gabby couldn't hold back laughter as their bowling game progressed. Every time Hank knocked pins down, he turned to her with a triumphant grim that made her resolve to beat him. She couldn't help it. There was something about the two of them that brought out the competitive spirit in each of them. Even Jess and Sam got into it, trying to beat each other. The four of them were comfortable enough with one another to make it hilarious.

"This time I'm going to do it; put me on top," said Hank, picking up his ball, standing at the head of the alley, and giving her a wicked grin.

"Sorry, bud, I've got it," said Sam. So far, he was the leader. But it was a close game which made them all want to do their best.

At the end, Sam was declared the winner, Gabby and Hank were tied for second place, and Jess shrugged off the teasing she got for coming in last. It was, Gabby decided, a congenial group of friends and a fun time.

After they finished their game, they went to one of the nightclubs for a drink before calling it a night.

In the club, bright lights flashed, and the beat of the loud music filled her ears. It had been a long time since she'd been in such surroundings. Gabby found herself tapping her toes as she sat next to Hank.

"Ready?" Hank asked her, and she quickly agreed.

Gabby was surprised by how well Hank danced. He effortlessly timed his movements to the tempo of the music and was light on his feet. And when a request came for something less demanding, he pulled her into his arms, and they moved easily together. She loved the different sides of himself he was showing her.

They finished their drinks, and then Sam and Jess announced they were leaving.

Hank gave her a questioning glance.

Gabby smiled, as ready for alone time with him as he.

Later, after making love, they lay side by side in his stateroom, talking.

"Can't wait to spend time with you back home," said Hank, caressing her cheek.

"I kept telling myself it would be wrong for us to date as long as we were both working for your father. I'm pleased that, with the changes awaiting us, that will no longer be an issue."

"So, I make you happy too?" he asked.

Gabby threw her arms around him and hugged him tightly. "You think?"

Chuckling, Hank said, "I'm going to continue staying in the house I bought in town. It's a short commute to the Mercedes dealership in Carrington."

"That makes sense," Gabby said.

"I didn't mind the long hours at work, but you're going to make it difficult for me," he teased, tucking a stray strand of hair behind her ear before he kissed her.

Gabby sank into the wanton feelings he brought out in her. *No wonder Ashley wanted to be with him,* Gabby thought dreamily, and then, alarmed, she sat up, ending their kiss. "Do you think Ashley will cause problems about our dating?"

"She has no right to do so, but she's unpredictable. Let's not worry about that now." Hank pulled her back into his arms, and though she relaxed in his embrace, a nagging feeling stayed with her. Ashley liked getting her way.

Chapter Ten

The next morning after being served breakfast in bed by Hank, Gabby rose and called Jess.

"You're going to go into St. Thomas with us?" Gabby asked her.

"Yes. Sam and I are eating breakfast with Ellie and John," said Jess.

"Okay, then, I'm going into our stateroom to get ready. I can't believe this is the last stop of the cruise. The time has flown by."

'It's been a whirlwind of activity, but so perfect," said Jess. "I'll join you in the stateroom in a short while."

Gabby clicked off the call, thinking back to the first day on the ship. She would never have guessed then what would happen to Jess and her. She hoped that their new relationships would remain strong once they were off the ship.

Charlotte Amalie, Gabby was told, is the capital of the U.S. Virgin Islands, and aside from its fabulous shopping, has a long history of pirates, including both Bluebeard and Blackbeard.

With two other cruise ships in the port, Gabby and her friends were just a few of many visitors ashore. Though the streets were crowded with shoppers, Gabby loved seeing all the wares at the different stores. Jewelry, cameras, watches, and electronics were just some of the duty-free goods.

Jess and Gabby finally agreed to meet the guys at a bar for lunch, giving them time to do some girl shopping without worrying about the men.

After much indecision, Gabby bought a pair of Tanzanite earrings in one store and a silver cuff with a 14k Gold link in another before buying more ordinary things like T-shirts and perfume. She found a sweet, soft, stuffed fish for Saree with a book to go along with it.

"I'm glad I waited to use my shopping funds until now," Jess told Gabby, gripping her packages.

"Me, too. I've really splurged, but I'm glad I could," Gabby replied.

Jess elbowed her. "Did you see all those beautiful engagement rings? It got me thinking about Sam and me. I hope this isn't just a shipboard romance. He says it isn't, but what if it turns out to be?" Her eyes filled with tears. "I've never felt this way about a man before."

"I've seen the way Sam looks at you, how he puts a protective hand on your back going through the crowds. I think you have something lasting."

Jess blew out a breath. "Yeah, I have to keep remembering that. He's very loyal to his grandmother. We've talked about the difficulties that may face us, but he's a polished, accomplished man who's never let anyone prevent him from succeeding."

"I know things have happened fast between you, but it doesn't mean it's wrong."

"How about you and Hank?" Jess asked.

"Hank and I have planned to continue seeing each other after we return to Ellenton. I want to take it slow, make sure things are the way they should be. He told me not to worry about Ashley, but I can't help it. That woman is bound to cause problems for us."

"Hank never looked at Ashley the way he looks at you," said Jess. "But you're right to want to be comfortable every step of the way." She checked her new watch. "It's time to meet the guys."

At a little outdoor restaurant, they ordered a variety of tacos they all shared and cool, frosted mugs filled with either beer or cokes.

"What have you guys been up to?" Jess asked Sam.

He glanced at Hank and back to her. "Hank and I pretty much stayed in one place focused on electronic gear. We knew you wouldn't want to hang with us. It looks like you did well for yourselves."

"Total splurge." Jess held out her hand so they could see the watch on her wrist.

"Cool. How about you, Gabby?" Hank asked.

Gabby showed them the bracelet and earrings she'd purchased. "Another total splurge. I'm calling them business accessories."

Hank laughed. "A true saleswoman."

They returned to the ship and spent the rest of the afternoon on board relaxing. Hank had already made dinner reservations for them at the NW Grille aboard the ship, an upscale restaurant featuring dishes inspired by The Pacific Northwest cuisine.

After relaxing by the pool, Gabby decided to go to her room to take a nap.

"You going to Hank's room?" Jess asked.

"I certainly can," Gabby answered, understanding what Jess wanted. Hank had given her the key to his stateroom, and rather than bother him in the casino with Sam, she went there.

Inside his room, she pulled the drapes closed, climbed atop the bed, and closed her eyes, her body embracing the languid feeling that came over her.

Sometime later, she felt movement beside her and awoke to see Hank lying beside her, propped on one elbow staring at her.

"Hi, beautiful," he murmured, drawing her closer.

She smiled into his blue-eyed gaze and reached up to touch his butterscotch hair, bleached by the sun. He looked like a poster boy for the cruise line, his ripped body, his handsome face relaxed.

"Did you have fun with Sam?" she asked, pleased they were becoming friends.

"I did. We both won some money. He's really talented at Blackjack. But after a while, I couldn't stop thinking of spending time with you."

He lowered his lips to hers, and she responded, loving the smell of him, the taste of him.

Much later, Gabby stood in the shower in her own stateroom, thinking about Hank. It seemed like a miracle that the man she'd been looking for all her life was someone she'd seen almost every day for the last year or so. Only now, away from the office, did she discover the man Hank truly was. He was handsome with an exciting, secure future ahead of him. But after spending hours talking to one another, it was Hank's vulnerability, his kindness, his softer side that drew her to him. Returning to work would be a challenge for them to keep their relationship out of it.

Though she was falling in love with Hank, her feelings about her work wouldn't change. She made substantial money at her job, enough that she didn't want to quit. More than that, she made individuals and families happy with their choice of safe, quality transportation. Dan Davis Dealerships were known throughout the area for their honesty and fairness. She could never work for a company she didn't respect.

Gabby put on one of the new dresses she'd bought for the trip. She'd finally been forced to recognize that the white dress she loved so much could never be worn again after Ashley threw red wine all over it. But her new, blue- flowered dress was perfect with her new earrings.

When she finally finished dressing and putting on

makeup, she stepped into the room to find Jess waiting for her with a glass of iced tea.

"Thought we could use this before we have cocktails and dinner. It's hard to believe the cruise is almost over. Where did the time go?"

Gabby clinked her glass of iced tea against Jess's glass, sending a happy tinkling sound into the room. "It's been more amazing than I'd hope. For both of us."

"Hear! Hear!" said Jess. "May this be the cruise that never ends in spirit."

Gabby faced Jess and returned her big smile. "Yes, I like that."

"Seriously, I feel good about you and Hank," said Jess. "It's convenient that you live in the same town. I know I won't be able to see Sam as much as you see Hank, but we're going to try to make it work."

"All we can do is take it one day at a time," said Gabby. "Things have happened fast for each of us."

"Yes, I know. That worries me," said Jess.

Inside the restaurant, the four of them chatted comfortably. Gabby found Sam so interesting, so sophisticated. From a young age, he'd traveled with his grandmother. And living in the city, he'd had many interesting experiences through friends of his grandfather. Though not as sophisticated, Jess had a way of bringing Sam to life with her gentle teasing, making him seem even more approachable. Like John with Ellie, Sam obviously adored Jess.

At one time, Gabby turned to find Hank's gaze on her. He smiled, sending waves of pleasure through her. He made her feel good about herself.

A waiter kept their wine glasses full as they went about eating their first course. Gabby had chosen a tomato broth with spicy lemongrass chicken, Hank selected Steak Tartare, and both Jess and Sam chose shrimp cocktail.

Gabby chose wild mushroom ravioli for her main course while the others chose filet mignon.

"Where's your grandmother tonight?" Gabby asked Sam.

"She's dining with Ellie and John. She's had a wonderful trip, meeting lots of people. But she enjoys Ellie the best. The people at the spa have been great for her, encouraging her to get out and move about more than usual. The warm weather and relaxed atmosphere help too."

"I've been encouraging her to write a book about all the interesting people she's met," said Jess. "She's had a fascinating life."

"Who knows? She might just do that. She's full of surprises," said Sam.

The waiter cleared their places then handed them a dessert menu.

"Each dessert choice looks wonderful," Jess said, grinning.

"I'm going to choose the Lemon-Brulee Tart with blueberry whipped cream and hope that the memory of it helps me get back on my regular diet," said Gabby.

"Superb idea," said Jess, laughing. "I'll go with the Baked Alaska."

The men decided on the Grand Marnier chocolate cake.

⚓

After dinner, the men wanted to go to one of the arcades.

"Okay with you?" Hank asked her.

"Sure." She loved video games as much as anyone else.

After an hour, she was ready for something quieter. "How about listening to the band?" she said to Hank.

"You wanna dance?" Hank said, grinning at her.

"Yes, I do." For as long as she lived, she'd remember dancing under the stars on the cruise ship with the man she'd already fallen for. It beat all the romantic PR pictures for cruises that she'd seen online.

They left the arcade and went to find the band. Couples of all ages were seated at tables listening to the music of the big band that was playing old songs from Benny Goodman and other musicians of the big band era.

The four of them were seated at a table near the dance floor.

Gabby loved watching the couples of all ages enjoy a variety of dances. Gabby eagerly got to her feet when Hank asked her to dance to a show tune. She was in the mood to keep the romance going. The real world was ashore, but she wanted to enjoy every moment aboard the ship.

As soft music flowed around and through them and

they swayed back and forth, Gabby became lost in the music and being in Hank's arms.

They were still dancing when Jess tapped on Gabby's shoulder. "Hey, you two, the music stopped a few minutes ago. Get a room."

Gabby and Hank looked at one another and laughed.

"Great idea," said Hank, offering his arm to Gabby.

Still chuckling, she took it and waved to Jess and Sam.

The next morning there was no time to lounge in bed after awakening at eight. She needed to quickly take a shower and finish packing so that the staff could pick up her suitcase outside the door of her stateroom.

As she dressed in layers in preparation to returning to cold, early-spring weather at home, she thought of all the possibilities going forward. Dan Davis had mentioned a new job for her. It would, no doubt, mean changes in her career and lifestyle. For the past few months, her life had been focused on work and dealing with the aftermath of her father's death. Now, her life was about to be made fuller by her relationship with Hank.

"I don't know if I can get everything into my suitcases," said Jess, groaning as she repacked one of her bags. "Do you have any room in yours?"

Gabby shook her head. "Not a spare inch. I shouldn't have bought the dress here on the ship, but I couldn't resist it." She barely managed to close her suitcase and stood. "I'll put mine outside. Do you need help with yours?"

"No, I'll manage. You'd better go ahead and grab something to eat at the buffet. I'm meeting Sam and Arabelle for coffee."

As Gabby left her room, she noticed Hank's luggage waiting outside the door to his stateroom. She hurried past. He'd promised to save her a seat at the buffet.

When she arrived, there was a crush of people moving through the area. Her stomach growled, and she knew Jess was right. She needed to eat a healthy meal now because she might not have another chance for some time while traveling.

She'd just finished loading her tray with food when she heard her name being called and looked up to see Hank waving at her.

She headed in his direction, happy to see him. She hadn't stayed the night with him because she wanted to spend time with Jess on their last night aboard the ship. Her winning tickets had given them the best vacation of their lives, but their friendship was the very foundation of it.

"Good morning," said Hank, rising and kissing her on the cheek. She smiled at him and wondered if this is what it might be like in the future, should they decide to move in together one day.

"Thanks for saving me a seat. It's more crowded than I thought it'd be."

"Everyone has the same idea of getting an early start to a day of travel," said Hank. "Too bad we're not on the same flight home."

"I'm spending the night at Jess's place before driving home the next day," Gabby said. "But I'll be at work bright and early the day after that, and then you'd better watch out! Can't wait to get going again."

He laughed. "We'll see what Dad has in mind."

After breakfast, they strolled the main deck. When Gabby saw Ellie and John, she hurried over to them. "Glad I have the chance to say goodbye. It was nice meeting you and spending time with you. Say hello to your granddaughters for me, and tell them I may surprise all of you with a visit to Florida."

Ellie beamed at her. "Weddings at the cove are exceptional."

Gabby laughed and hugged her. "You never know," she whispered. "Thanks for your nudge into seeing something might be right about Hank and me."

She hugged John. "Thanks for teaching us a little about wine. I'll be more adventuresome in the future."

He grinned. "Superb wine and delicious food are blessings not to be ignored."

Hank said his goodbyes to them, and they left to find Jess and Sam.

They found them with Arabelle in a cozy spot toward the stern of the ship. Gabby waved and approached them. "Arabelle, I'm so glad I had the chance to see you again. I've enjoyed your company and want to wish you the best in the future."

"Thank you, my dear," Arabelle said. "It's been a

pleasure. Ellie's trying to get all of us to Florida one day. Who knows? It may happen."

Hank and Sam started talking.

Arabelle held out her hand, and Jess took it. "Now that it's just us girls, I want to say how much I've enjoyed seeing Sam so happy. You both are invited to my home in the city anytime. The two of you are delightful." She turned to Gabby. "I like what I see of those two."

Jess's cheeks turned a bright pink as her eyes filled. "Thank you. That means so much to me."

"Looks like we're getting close to land," said Hank. "I'm going to my room to make sure I got everything."

"Wise idea," said Gabby. "Want me to check for you too, Jess?"

"Thanks," Jess said, giving her a grateful look.

Gabby headed back to the room, aware that Jess wanted every minute she could with Sam and Arabelle. She didn't blame her. Life after the cruise would be different for all of them.

Chapter Eleven

The transition from peaceful, lazy cruise days to the real world was a shock for both Gabby and Jess as they finally sat on a plane headed to New York.

"Whew! For a minute, I didn't think we were going to make the flight," said Jess, buckling her seatbelt.

"Hard to realize the members of the mob departing the ship were all aboard with us. With so many places to be, the ship didn't seem that crowded," said Gabby, tucking her purse and carry-on beneath the seat in front of her. "Thank heavens, we're flying first class." After the cruise was over, the magic of her winning tickets prevailed with these seats.

Gabby leaned back in her chair and closed her eyes. She gripped the armrests beside her. "Do you feel as if the ship is still moving?"

"Yes," said Jess. She laughed. "At first, I thought it was the way Sam always makes me feel when he puts his arms around me."

"I hope the two of you make it back together on land," said Gabby seriously.

"Me, too," said Jess. "But I have no reason to think we won't. Sam isn't a player, and Arabelle would never encourage us if she were against it. Arabelle knows what we're up against by some. But I'd like to think people are more open now."

"I would hope so," said Gabby.

"But we know racism hasn't magically disappeared," said Jess. "My sisters have faced challenges in their relationships because of it."

"If anyone reacts negatively, you don't want them around you," said Gabby.

"I know," Jess said.

Gabby closed her eyes again. Disregarding the motion that she still felt from being at sea, she settled her thoughts on Hank. The atmosphere of being on a cruise had made it easier for her to relax her natural caution in romantic encounters, but then she'd known and admired Hank before the trip, just not in a romantic way. But now that she knew the man intimately, she was hooked. He was kind, gentle, sweet, and funny. And almost as good a salesperson as she.

A limo pre-arranged as part of the ticket package picked them up at the airport and drove them to Jess's apartment. Standing on the curb, her suitcase and carry-ons around her, Gabby made a snap decision.

"Do you mind if I don't stay the night?" she asked

Jess after helping her get her suitcases inside the building. "I'm suddenly anxious to get back home. We can decompress on the phone."

"Not at all. Sam planned to call me later, and I have a lot to do to get ready for work tomorrow. I can't thank you enough for taking me on this trip." Jess gave her a hug. "I want to save some special time for us to talk after we get things settled."

"That's a deal."

Gabby rolled her suitcase along the sidewalk, pleased to see her car untouched where she'd parked it. She loaded her bags inside, and waving once more to Jess, who'd stepped outside to see her off, she started the engine. After being away, she couldn't wait to get back to her own space.

Later, as she pulled into the driveway of her three-story townhome, she felt as if she truly was coming home. Until now, this place had seemed a refuge from sadness, but now it seemed full of possibilities.

After bringing her bags inside, Gabby took a look around. She'd kept a few things from the home she'd shared with her dad, mostly sentimental items, and had selected a whole new style of furnishings different from the old-fashioned colonial pieces she'd known in their house.

Now comfortable country furniture filled the rooms, inviting people to relax and enjoy. The rich dark color of wooden pieces was softened by the cream-and-gray color scheme she'd chosen, accented with brighter colors here and there.

Gabby sighed with happiness, turned on music to fill

the house, and took her luggage into her bedroom on the first-floor to unpack.

As she lifted her clothes out of the suitcase, each article of clothing inspired a memory of her vacation. The cruise had been the trip of a lifetime for her. And now that she'd gone on it, she wanted to do a lot more traveling. She loved the idea that selling vehicles would provide her with wheels of her own to take her to new, intriguing places.

She hugged a dress to her and began to sway to the music, recalling how wonderful it had felt to be in Hank's arms. She'd just twirled around when her cell rang. *Hank.*

"Hi. Are you back home?"

"Yes, I just wanted to make sure you got to Jess's place all right," he said.

"I'm home. I wanted to have some extra time to get things settled here before returning to work."

"I'm going into the office tomorrow, but I understand you're not due in until the day after," said Hank. "Is that still the plan?"

"Yes. Though if Dan needs me, I can arrange to come in earlier."

"Maybe tomorrow night we could go out to dinner."

"That sounds great, Hank. I'd like that."

"Okay then, that's what we'll do. See you tomorrow night." He paused. "I'm already missing you, Gabby."

At his words, pleasure filled her. "Me too."

After she ended the call, she went back to dancing, but it wasn't the same after hearing Hank's voice and knowing he was in the same town and yet, so far away.

The next morning, Gabby awoke and stared at her surroundings—familiar yet jarring to see. She'd been dreaming of being on the cruise ship with Hank. She stared out at the gray, cold weather and got out of bed bent on making this day of recovery count. She would do laundry, grocery shopping, and go over her personal finances to prepare for the rest of the workweek. Now that she was inspired to do more traveling, she intended to perform even better at her job.

She was in her robe doing laundry when the doorbell rang. Frowning, she went to see who it might be at this early hour. She looked through the peephole in the door, grinned, and opened the door. "Good morning, Hank. What brings you here?"

"You." He handed her a hot cup from the local coffee shop. "I was going to come last night, but I thought it better if I gave you some time to get settled. But this morning, I couldn't wait any longer."

He took the coffee from her, set it on the hall table, and tugged her into his arms. "I've missed you," he murmured and lowered his lips to hers.

The feel of him, the smell of him, brought back blissful moments with him on the ship. She responded, eager for him to know how much she'd missed him.

When they finally pulled apart, they beamed at one another.

"I had to prove to myself that what I felt with you was real and that you felt it too," said Hank.

"I dreamt of you, us, last night," Gabby confessed.

"We've got to make sure what we have will work both in our private lives and on the job," said Hank. "Dad's setting up a staff meeting for the whole crew, both dealerships, tomorrow morning. Do I have your permission to tell him about us?"

"Yes, I think he should know, but we shouldn't make a big deal out of it to the rest of the company. Agreed?

"That makes sense." Hank checked his watch. "Guess I'd better go. Can't be late my first day back."

They kissed once more. Then Gabby stood by the door and waved him off, then went into the kitchen with the forgotten cup of coffee. While she heated it up, she called Jess to wish her a happy day back at work.

"Hey, there," said Jess. "I was about to call you. Are you still taking the day off?"

"Yes, but tomorrow morning there's a company-wide meeting. I'm not sure what that's about. Did Sam call you last night?"

"Yes," said Jess. "But he was in a hurry and said his time would be more limited, but he'd try to call as often as he could. He'll get his new schedule, and we'll go from there."

"Sounds reasonable," Gabby said, though she could hear the disappointment in Jess's voice.

They chatted a while longer, and then Gabby went back to her list of things to do.

That afternoon, Gabby was surprised to receive a call from Hank's father.

"Hello, Mr. Davis," she said, wondering why he was calling her.

"Welcome back, Gabby," he said cheerfully. "I believe Hank has told you about a company-wide meeting set for tomorrow morning. I thought it only fair that we get together for a private talk before then. Are you available to meet me at the Lexus dealership and then to join Hank and me for a business dinner?"

"Yes," she answered. "May I ask why?"

"Of course. It's something that I think will make you happy. I'd rather not give the details to you until we meet. Shall we say six o'clock?"

"That sounds fine," said Gabby, her mind racing. She'd have enough time to shampoo her hair and take a shower.

Gabby walked into the Lexus dealership feeling as if she was coming home. She loved seeing the shiny new cars, the sparkling offices, the pleasant lounge for customers waiting for their cars to be serviced.

As soon as she approached her office, she knew something was wrong. Her name had been removed from the glass door. A closer look told her that her personal items were no longer there. Her pulse began to race. *Was she going to be told she'd lost her job? No, Dan had said she'd be happy.*

Hank appeared. "Hi, Gabby. Don't worry about this." He indicated the office with a wave of his hand. He gave her a quick, almost furtive kiss and took her arm. "Come with me to Dad's new office."

"His new office?" said Gabby. "What happened to his old one?"

"Later," Hank said and led her inside a space that had been set up for Dan.

Smiling, Dan rose to his feet and held out his hand. "Gabby, so nice to see you. It looks like the vacation was a good one. You look terrific, well-rested, and ready to get back to work."

"Thanks. I am. You know I love working here," she said, still puzzled about the changes that had taken place while she was gone.

"Have a seat," said Dan, indicating one of the two chairs in front of his desk.

She sat in one, Hank in the other.

From behind his desk, he smiled at them. "My two best salespeople. I can't wait to see what the year ahead will bring for both this dealership and the Mercedes dealership in Carrington. With the two of you helping to run them, it's going to be a challenge to see who does better while I begin to enjoy more time away from this business and begin a new enterprise of my own."

"You're leaving the dealerships?" Gabby said, shocked.

"Not exactly. I'm taking on a more executive position over the two of you. That is, if you'll accept my offer to manage the staff of the Lexus dealership while continuing to sell cars."

Hank turned to her. "He's given me the same offer in Carrington."

"What exactly does the new job involve if I'm to continue selling cars?" Gabby asked.

"You have an excellent way of managing people. I've watched as you've encouraged other salespeople and spoken to both new and old customers. I need to be able to stop worrying about my staff and concentrate on making each place more profitable, even offering more benefits to my employees. Does that make sense?"

"Yes, it does," said Gabby. "I have a few ideas about how to change things up a bit."

"You do?" said Dan, looking amused.

Gabby grinned. "I was saving them for my next job evaluation."

Dan laughed. "Okay, we can talk about that later. Let's make no mistake here. You and Hank are in competition. At the end of the year, an award will be given to the winner."

Hank and Gabby exchanged challenging looks. Gabby could feel the excitement build inside her. She loved a close contest.

"On another note," Dan said. "I understand it's a smart idea to have you two working in separate environments to comply with my dating rules."

Gabby felt her cheeks grow hot.

Hank leaned over and took her hand in his. "Dad knows all about the fiasco with Ashley and our dating."

"And I like it," Dan said. "I had a feeling something like this might happen under the right circumstances."

Gabby looked at Hank and laughed. "He sounds like Ellie Rizzo."

"Guess he's as bad," Hank said, shaking his head at his father.

"What's this all about?" Dan asked.

"Destiny," said Gabby, realizing how true it might be.

"Well, let's go to dinner," said Dan, standing. "I'm hungry. Tomorrow, I'll give you the details, Gabby. You'll be getting a substantial raise, of course. With your approval, I'll announce the change tomorrow morning at the meeting after we've had the opportunity to seal the deal."

"Thank you. I'm very excited about this offer. What about my office?"

"We've already moved your things into my old office. Your name and new title have been painted on the door."

Gabby's eyes widened, and then she laughed. "That confident, huh?"

Dan returned her smile. "It's perfect for you. Your father would be so proud."

Gabby smiled, knowing Dan was right. She could almost hear her father say, "Well done, Gabrielle, my belle."

She ignored the sting in her eyes as she shook hands with Dan.

Tony's food was as delicious as the simplicity of their surroundings. Gabby sat with Hank and Dan, enjoying a bowl of pasta Bolognese. After being away for almost two weeks and eating delicious meals, Gabby was grateful for the opportunity to continue having food as wonderful as this before she returned to her usual, simpler diet.

Dan took a sip of his glass of Chianti and then said, "Now that we're away from the office, I can speak frankly about the two of you dating. I couldn't be more delighted. Your father and I used to talk about it when having a beer after work. But, of course, we never mentioned it to either of you for fear that it would put an end to the idea."

"But I didn't know Hank until recently," said Gabby. "What made you think it would happen?"

"Because I knew Hank and your father knew you," Dan said, chuckling. "As pleased as I am, it's important that the two of you not let your relationship interfere with your work. That wouldn't be fair to the other staff members. That's why I have such a hard and fast rule about it. Ours is a competitive business, and each sales-person deserves to be given a fair chance to make it on his or her own."

"I agree, Dad," said Hank. "But I'm not going to let Gabby and her crew do better than me and mine."

"That's exactly what I like about the two of you together," said Dan, winking at them.

"Ellie would be impressed," said Gabby, and she and Hank laughed together.

Chapter Twelve

The next morning, Gabby arrived before the dealership opened and got her office settled, with everything from pens to sales applications placed how she liked them. Dan had surprised her with new business cards. Seeing them, she was aware of how well Dan knew her. Yes, he'd mentioned a new position for her, but that's all he'd said.

Dan came to her office. "Ready to talk details?"

At the end of the meeting, she didn't know who was more pleased, she or Dan. She liked her raise and the responsibilities he was giving her, and Dan liked that she already had several ideas she wanted to implement.

Later, during the meeting in the dealership's conference room, Gabby was touched to see the pleasure of her sales group when it was announced that she was taking over the newly created position of Sales Personnel Manager.

"Thank you, everyone. I'm delighted to be able to help you and become a support to you. I'm always open to suggestions, so don't hesitate to talk to me anytime about any issue you might have. We at the Lexus dealership are going to have a very successful year."

Hank winked at her from his seat across the room with his salespeople. Earlier, he'd more or less told them the same thing.

A sense of fun filled Gabby. They'd be in competition, but it would keep both Hank and her on their toes. There was nothing like a challenge between them to keep the nighttime sparks flaming.

After the meeting, Hank walked over to her. "May the best person, the best team win."

"Indeed," she said, grinning. She had every intention of doing so.

Hank laughed. "I love it when you get that gleam in your eye."

She joined in. "As I said, it's going to be a good year."

Over the next few days, Gabby set up an attractive display on the wall in the showroom next to the line of offices. She'd had a professional sign made—a brass plate mounted on a walnut background said EMPLOYEES OF THE MONTH. Two identical wooden frames were mounted on the plaque below it. A brass plate beneath one frame said "Salesperson"; the other said "Service Rep."

When Dan saw it, he gave her a look of approval. "Love the idea. We don't give our service people enough credit, do we?"

"The reliable ones? No," she replied. Her father had told her that mechanics working on the cars, preparing them for buyers, then servicing them later were an unseen and sometimes forgotten asset to the business. She was committed to making sure that didn't happen under her supervision.

"Did you notice the new sign in the waiting room?" she asked.

At his head shake, she took his arm and led him to it.

Above a coffee/tea/cocoa service table, she'd had a sign hung that said: Welcome. Please relax and enjoy our hospitality while our service department takes care of you.

"Very nice," said Dan giving her a look of approval. "I like the additions of the plants and a small refrigerator by the service table too."

"The plants aren't real, but it does soften the room a bit. Also, I've set up a sales case with Lexus items for customers to buy." Baseball hats in white, black, and tan, with the Lexus logo, were displayed along with a variety of T-shirts and mugs. "We want our owners to share the news."

Dan laughed softly. "I had no idea you'd move so quickly, but I'm glad you did." He gazed around. "This room looks so much better with a few touches like yours."

"I want to talk to you about hiring an additional part-time salesman for the weekends. His brother owns a Lexus bought here, and he's very enthusiastic about Lexus and us."

"Okay," said Dan. "Bring him in for an interview, and you can introduce me to him."

"Okay. He's already sent me his resume." Gabby loved her new role.

"I'm going to review the financial and sales reports, now. We can talk about any new hires later," said Dan. He gave her a little salute and walked away.

Pleased, Gabby went into her office to work on a few promotions she was developing. She was typing up a report when there was a knock on her door. She looked up and held in a gasp when she saw Ashley standing there.

"Hello, Ashley."

Ashley gave her a cold look and gazed around the office. "I see it didn't take you long to move into the family's business by screwing the boss's son. Just like it didn't take you long to move into my stateroom on the ship after I left."

Gabby got to her feet. "What do you want, Ashley? Why are you here?"

She placed a hand on her hip. "I came to see Hank. I was told he no longer worked here."

"No, he doesn't." Gabby didn't say more. She hated conflict and had no intention of arguing with Ashley.

"Well, I guess I'll have to go visit him at the Mercedes dealership. He's going to realize we both made a mistake, but there's still time to get back together before my sister's wedding. I was taking a lot of medication, so I wasn't responsible for what I said or did."

Gabby was trying to figure out what to say when Ashley stepped closer. "You may think you've attracted Hank, but just wait and see. I know how happy we were together."

"If you were so-o-o happy together, why did Hank break up with you?" Gabby countered.

Ashley glared at her. "It's a misunderstanding, that's all. We're getting back together."

"Okay." Gabby stared at her. "What does that have to do with me?"

Ashley's eyes narrowed. "Don't get in my way."

"Wouldn't dream of it. As a matter of fact, this might be a good time for you to leave." Gabby pointed at the door.

Ashley turned on her heel and made her way across the showroom floor, ignoring the looks other people gave her.

Unsettled, Gabby sank onto her desk chair and took a couple of deep breaths to calm herself. She was tempted to call Hank but decided not to. He'd have to face Ashley on his own. It was their business, not hers. But that didn't stop a thread of worry from weaving inside her.

A couple of hours later, she received a call from Hank. "Guess who came to see me?"

"If you're talking about Ashley, she visited here earlier," said Gabby.

"Ashley announced she'd been to visit the Lexus dealership and told you off. Then she explained she didn't mean all the things she said or did, that she was on medication. I told her she was crazy to think we'd ever get back together, that I was sorry the cruise turned out to be miserable for her, but it was irretrievably over between us."

Gabby could hear the anger that lingered in his voice. "How did she respond?"

"She told me I'd be sorry, that you were nothing but a loser and always had been." He let out a laugh that had no humor. "She obviously doesn't know you. Who won the tickets for the cruise? It wasn't me. Who's in charge of the Lexus dealership? I understand why you and Jess never liked her. In the time I knew her, Ashley was very careful to hide her true nature from me."

"She can be very clever about controlling her mean streak," said Gabby. "I'm going to keep on staying away from her. I don't need or want her in my life."

"Yeah, me too," said Hank. "I told her if she popped up at the Lexus or Mercedes dealerships again, we'd file protective orders against her. We don't need to be harassed. She left in a hurry, but Ashley got the message. I realize now that Ashley and I never had a chance to talk, really talk to one another. She always had some activity planned to prevent that. I'm sorry. I was so ..."

Gabby cut him off. "No need to apologize. Like you said, it's over, and we can move forward."

"Thanks, Gabby. I'm so glad we had the chance to get to know one another."

"It just took two winning tickets to do it," said Gabby, attempting to add humor to the situation.

He laughed. "I'm really glad now that you won them. Want to have dinner together after work?"

"I'm going to babysit Saree, my little sister, tonight. You can come with me if you'd like."

"What time?"

"Seven o'clock. Her parents are going to a movie. I can't wait to see her and give her the stuffed fish and book I bought for her in St. Thomas."

"Why don't I pick up a pizza and bring it to your house before we go see Saree? Keep it simple," suggested Hank.

"That would be great," Gabby said. "And, Hank, I appreciate your willingness to spend time with Saree. That's nice of you."

"I've heard you talk about her. I'll be happy to meet her because she's part of your life."

"Thanks. I don't do enough community work, but this is one little thing I can do," said Gabby. Giving Saree's foster parents a break was a rewarding way to give back.

That evening, Gabby gazed around her house, checking to make sure everything was in order. This was the first time Hank would see more than the front entry, and she wanted him to like it. She was very proud of the townhouse she'd bought on her own. It sat in a very nice development that abutted a copse of trees on one side and a golf course on the other.

Hank arrived on schedule carrying a pizza box and wearing a broad grin when she opened the door to greet him.

"'Evening. Come on in," she said, standing back and holding the door for him.

He stepped inside, leaned over to give her a quick kiss, and followed her into the kitchen. "This is nice. I like it," said Hank. "Easier to handle than the house I bought from Dad."

"Your father's house, now yours, is beautiful," said Gabby. Hank's house was in Hilltop, an upscale neighborhood that sat on the edge of town next to Carrington.

Gabby brought out a couple of cans of Coke. "Here you go. I make it a policy not to have any alcohol on my breath when I see Saree because her condition was caused by her mother's abuse of alcohol."

"No problem. I understand," said Hank. "Tell me more about Saree and her foster family."

"Rich and Ronnie Billings are super nice. They have two boys of their own—ten-year-old Aaron and Jake, who is eight. They wanted to add a little girl to the family, but Ronnie can't have more children, so when they looked to adopt, they learned about children like Saree, who were considered unadoptable. They decided to foster her."

"How behind is Saree?" Hank asked.

"At three, she's just starting to walk now, and though she can hear and see, she doesn't talk clearly. She's hyperactive with a short attention span, which makes it difficult to spend time on any projects with her. She's a sweet little girl, though, who loves to cuddle despite everything else."

"It sounds like a tough situation for the foster parents," Hank commented.

"They're wonderful with her. Saree has made a lot of progress since they took her in a year or so ago. It is draining, however, which is why I like to give them time to go out whenever they can manage it. Their boys also are wonderful with Saree. She's a very lucky little girl to be with them."

"And they're lucky to have you to step in every once

in a while," said Hank wrapping an arm around her and kissing her on the cheek.

Gabby served up the pizza, and they sat at the kitchen bar eating quietly. Gabby was thrilled Hank was interested in Saree. She'd already called Ronnie to ask for permission to bring him along.

Promptly at seven, Gabby drove up in front of the Billings' house, a cute Cape Cod that was well-maintained with a fenced yard both in front and in back, as Gabby had previously discovered.

Hank followed her to the front door.

Clutching the bag of packages she'd wrapped earlier, Gabby rang the bell and waited.

Ronnie opened the door, looking harried. Her dark hair was pulled back in a ponytail, and she hadn't taken the time to put on any makeup. But the smile that crossed her face when she saw Gabby and Hank made her beautiful features light up.

As Gabby and Hank entered the house, Rich joined them. "Glad you could make it. You know how much we appreciate your help." He was of average height, a little overweight, but with a friendly openness that attracted people to him.

"You look terrific," Ronnie said. "The cruise must have been outstanding."

"Thanks, it was, in part because of this guy. This is Hank Davis," Gabby said. "A special friend."

Hank bobbed his head to Ronnie, and then he and Rich shook hands.

Gabby reached into her bag and brought out a small, wrapped box. "This is for you, Ronnie. Something I brought back from the cruise."

Tears filled Ronnie's eyes. "Thank you, Gabby. That was so thoughtful."

"I hope you'll like it. You can't imagine how many perfumes I smelled to get the right one for you."

Ronnie laughed. "Thanks. Now, you have a little girl waiting in the living room to see her Bee."

"Bee?" Hank said.

"She can't say Gabby. It comes out as Bee," explained Ronnie.

When Gabby walked into the room, Saree lifted her arms from her place on the floor. Tears stung Gabby's eyes. She picked up the little girl and hugged her. "Hi, Saree, sweetheart."

Saree patted Gabby's cheeks. "Bee."

Gabby turned to Ronnie. "You've done so much work with her in the almost three weeks I've been gone."

Rich put his arm around Ronnie. "The best teacher in the world."

Aaron and Jake joined them. "Hi, Gabby," they said, speaking in a chorus.

"Hi, boys. Meet my friend, Hank."

"Hello," said Aaron. At ten and eight, both he and his younger brother were strong, athletic-looking boys with their father's brown hair and blue eyes.

"Nice to meet you," Jake said.

Gabby held up the bag. "There are presents for you inside." She walked to the couch and sat down, holding onto Saree, who was squirming to get down. She gave the boys each a gift and then lifted the stuffed fish out to give to Saree.

Saree studied the fish.

Gabby took Saree's hand and touched her fingers to the soft surface of the fish.

A smile crossed Saree's face.

Gabby tucked the fish into Saree's arms and faced Rich and Ronnie. "The fish comes with a storybook that I'll read to her later if I can."

"Nice," said Ronnie, giving her a grateful look.

"Thanks, Gabby," said Aaron holding up a gray T-shirt that said St. Thomas on it.

"Mine's cool, too," Jake said, placing his yellow T-shirt against his chest.

"I'm glad." She'd been careful to avoid any T-shirts with crude sayings on them and had chosen simple, tropical scenes.

"It looks almost like Christmas around here," said Rich.

"I didn't forget you," said Gabby. She reached inside the bag and brought out a mug for Rich. "For either coffee or beer."

Rich laughed. "Got me covered morning and night, huh? Thanks so much."

Hank had been standing by, but now he took a seat next to Gabby on the couch.

"We'd better leave while Saree is occupied," said Ronnie. "She's all ready for bed anytime you can get her down. See you later. We should be back before eleven."

"Take your time," said Gabby. She kept Saree's attention with the fish while Ronnie and Rich quietly left.

"You boys play sports?" Hank asked them.

"In the spring and summer. Not the winter," said Aaron. "How are you at video games?

Hank grinned. "Depends. What do you have in mind?"

"Marvel's Avengers," said Aaron, giving him a hopeful look.

"Try me," said Hank. He stood and turned to Gabby. "I'll help keep the boys occupied. Let me know if you need help with Saree." He bent and kissed Gabby's cheek and then gently touched Saree's cheek with one finger.

Saree studied him but didn't turn away.

After Hank and the boys left the room, Gabby took out the board book about a fish and started to read it. Saree was interested in it for only a few minutes, then began to fuss.

Eager to see how Saree was doing walking, she set her on the floor and held her hands. "Shall we walk?" she said softly.

Saree took off heading for the kitchen, moving her little legs with more and more sureness, letting out a squeal of joy as she did.

Thrilled, Gabby allowed Saree to guide her.

When Saree began to tire, Gabby lifted her up and hugged her. "Good girl. Soon you'll be running."

Saree faced her and patted her cheek.

Gabby carried her back to the couch to see if they could read another page or two of the storybook.

Holding the fish, Saree looked at the pictures Gabby

showed her and then pounded the book with her fist and began to cry.

Gabby carried Saree to her room and sat down in the rocking chair with her. She knew from past experiences that too much stimulation was exhausting for her. It was close to bedtime anyway.

Humming softly, Gabby rocked Saree back and forth, waiting for her to settle down. It was never a quick process. The little girl would seem to relax, then tense up and let out a little cry. Finally, Saree's eyelids closed, and her body relaxed.

Gabby sat watching her, rocking her, wondering what it would be like to have a child of her own. With Hank. Chiding herself for thinking of such a thing when they'd only begun dating,

On the way back to her townhouse so that Hank could get his car, Gabby turned to him. "You're awfully good with kids. Do you want a big family one day?"

"With you? Then yes," His lips curved. "You're such a natural mother with Saree, and the boys obviously love you too."

"As an only child, having children is important to me."

"I think three is a nice number," said Hank. "Seeing the two boys and one girl tonight, it seemed like a perfect combination."

"I think so too," said Gabby, more than pleased with his response. Any man in her life had to like the idea of having a family with her. She'd always been sorry she'd never had siblings.

She pulled up in front of her home. "Guess we'd better call it a night. I've got to get up early tomorrow morning for a staff meeting I've called."

"Okay, but I hope to spend more time with you another night."

She parked the car, and they both got out.

Hank came over to her and pulled her into his arms. She wrapped her arms around him and lifted her face for the kiss she knew was coming.

Hank's lips met hers in a warm, comforting kiss that quickly turned into something hotter, more demanding. She responded, then stepped back.

"Maybe tomorrow night, you can spend time here."

He grinned. "Have a successful meeting tomorrow. I've already met with my staff today."

She laughed at his teasing tone. No question, they were in competition.

Chapter Thirteen

The next morning, Gabby went into the office early as she'd told Hank she would. Even though the meeting would be brief, she wanted to be well-prepared. She would announce the salesperson and the service person of the month and talk about what qualities would be required for those awards. She'd also received an agreement from Dan that a monetary reward of $500 would be given to each winner. She knew how much that would mean to some of the staff and figured it was money well-spent.

People gathered in the conference room on time.

Gabby began the meeting with a discussion about the monthly awards. As expected, a buzz of excitement filled the room.

"And now, I want to talk about ownership here at the dealership. It's not about actually owning it but owning your job here and treating this place of business as if it were yours to show off. That means when you see something that needs to be done, take care of it. Our receptionist is not to be considered your servant. If your customers want a cold drink, water, or coffee, get it for them instead of asking Jen. If something is out of place in the visitor lounge, take care of it. Fixing a stack of magazines, placing an empty cup in the trash bin or the like is something we all can do to make this place something you're proud of. Own that piece of belonging."

Among the murmuring that followed, Gabby heard agreement. "Remember, I'm here to make any sale go easier for you if I can be of assistance. We're all competing against one another, but we're all here to help each other too."

"How do I know I can trust another salesperson not to steal my prospect?" asked a new salesman.

"If anything like that happens, the person in question will be fired immediately. Dan Davis is all about fairness and allowing each of us an equal chance to make a sale."

The meeting went on longer than expected, but by the end, Gabby was glad they'd been able to talk freely. When she returned to her desk, she was pleased that the group was coming together nicely.

That afternoon as Gabby was about ready to end her day at the dealership, Hank called. "How about coming to my house for dinner? I want you to see my place. I'll order Chinese?"

"That sounds tasty. I like most anything, so whatever you want to order is fine with me." She ended the call, packed up, and left work eager to see Hank's home.

Driving up in front of the large two-story house of white-clapboards with dark-green shutters flanking the front windows, Gabby thought it a stately home that seemed welcoming at the same time. Lush landscaping and tall trees gave a sense of privacy to the space around it. Buds were showing on some of the deciduous trees, and a flowering dogwood tree in front of the house was exhibiting early signs of springtime flowering.

As she got out of her car in the front circle, Hank opened the door and walked out to greet her. "Hello! Welcome to my abode."

She grinned and went into his open arms. "All it needs is a big dog running to greet me or, perhaps, a little dachshund."

"Ah, a dog lover. Great. I've wanted a dog but haven't figured out how to work it with my schedule. Maybe sometime in the future. And why a dachshund?"

"Jess's family had one when we were growing up, and I loved her. Lucy was her name. She was so smart and funny, too. Believe me, she used to run their busy household."

Hank wrapped an arm around her and led her to the front door. "Maybe someday, we can do that together. Come in. We have time for a glass of wine and a look around before our dinner will be delivered."

Gabby stepped into the black-and-white-tiled entry and paused. To her right, a living room held a white-washed brick fireplace and comfortable seating with two couches and several soft-cushioned chairs placed strategically in the room. To the left of the hallway, a formal dining room held a stunning mahogany dining room table surrounded by eight chairs and a matching sideboard.

Farther down the hall beyond the living room was a rich, wood-paneled library and a small guest bathroom.

The dining room, she discovered, was separated from the kitchen with a butler's pantry. Hank explained that the kitchen had been recently remodeled. Dark-gray marble counters, white cupboards, and the latest in kitchen equipment were part of it. In the center, a working island had four bar stools drawn up to it. A kitchen table and four chairs sat in an area by French doors leading outside to a covered porch and beyond it to a pool.

She turned to him with a smile. "This is a beautiful house. You must be so proud to own it."

"It's a little big for just one person, but it's a great house for later. That's why I agreed to buy it from Dad. He didn't want it to leave the family. C'mon, there's more to see."

Upstairs, to the right, three bedrooms were comfortably arranged. One with an ensuite bathroom, the other two separated by a Jack and Jill bathroom.

To the left, a large master bedroom was empty. Surprised, Gabby stopped. "Why no furniture?"

"I'm waiting for the right moment to furnish it. My dad was sentimental about the room, remembering happy, earlier times with my mother. I'm waiting to furnish it until the timing is right. But come in. It's my favorite room in the house. Look up. At night you can see the stars through the skylight. During the day, you can see the tops of the trees."

Gabby studied it. "Yes, it's like living in the trees. Beautiful. You should paint the walls green like the color of new leaves in the spring."

Hank showed her the master bath, closet, and dressing room, and then they went back downstairs.

In the kitchen, Hank opened a bottle of wine and poured them each a glass. They sat at the kitchen island facing one another.

Hank lifted her hand and squeezed it. "I'm glad you like the house. I know it needs some final touches here and there, but it's got all the basics."

"It's a lovely home," said Gabby. "It has a lot of charm with little finishing touches like unique wood trim that you don't get in new construction."

The doorbell rang, ending their conversation. Hank went to the door and returned shortly with a big bag of food from Gabby's favorite Chinese restaurant.

Hank put a plate, napkin, and silverware in front of their places and opened all the boxes.

"So much food, and it all smells yummy," said Gabby.

"Guess I got carried away, but I wasn't sure which might be your favorite." He brought out several serving spoons. "Help yourself."

Gabby took a sample of each thing. Later, she wasn't sure which she'd enjoyed more— the vegetable medley, the Orange Chicken, Moo Shu Pork, or the other three choices. Each was delicious.

"Thanks. You'll have plenty left over for lunch," she said.

He grinned. "Or another dinner. It makes it easy that way. Do you like to cook?"

She loved that they were still curious about one another. "Not when I'm alone. But I grew to love cooking for my dad growing up. He was a good cook himself and taught me the basics. Occasionally, I still get a creative urge and want to do something unique."

"I get it. But you're too busy winning tickets to cruises," Hank teased.

Gabby laughed. "Are you ever going to let me forget it?"

"Nope. It was my lucky day when you won them. Look what's happening between us."

She grinned at him, as happy as he that they were together.

"Let's go sit by the fire," said Hank. He grabbed the bottle of wine and his glass and carried them into the living room.

Gabby followed him with her own wine glass, content with both the meal and, more importantly, being with him.

They sat on the couch in front of the fireplace.

Gabby took a sip of wine and stared at the flames flickering in the fireplace, becoming mesmerized by the changing light.

Hank put his arm around her. "Have I told you lately that I've fallen in love with you?" He took the wine glass from her hand, set it down, and lowered his lips to hers.

Desire filled her with need. As they kissed, she knew she wanted to make this relationship work. She hadn't said those three special words to him, but she already felt deep love for him. Something true and emotional. Something she'd never felt before.

When they pulled apart, Hank clasped her face in his hands and settled his gaze on her. "I love you, Gabby."

Overcome by the tender way he spoke, the way he'd opened up to her, tears of joy threatened to fill Gabby's eyes. What they'd found with one another was the thing of dreams, the stories she read so eagerly.

"I love you, too," she said softly, squeezing him tighter. "I know it happened quickly, but I've been waiting all this time to find you."

She snuggled up against him, secure in his arms.

Chapter Fourteen

The next morning, Gabby called Jess.

"How are things going?" she asked, wondering if Jess and Sam were still seeing one another.

"Great," said Jess. "How about you? How are things with you and Hank?"

"We're in love," Gabby said as a tingle went through her body at the memory of making love last night.

"Oh, Gabby, I'm so happy for you," gushed Jess. "Sam and I are still seeing each other, our feelings haven't changed, but it's a struggle to find quality time together. We're still working on it. Who knew a Caribbean cruise could be so magical for both of us?"

"I know. Remember, the name of our ship was Tropical Magic. We certainly found ours, didn't we?"

Jess let out a happy chuckle. "It is sort of magic, huh? I'm meeting Arabelle for lunch next weekend. I'm showing her how to facetime Ellie."

"Oh, sweet! Say hi to both for me." Gabby checked

the time. "I'd better go. Did you like the text I sent you about Ashley?"

"So typical of her. I'm glad that Hank put her in her place. I'm sure she didn't like the mention of a restraining order. Ashley would be mortified if that got out. Serves her right. Keep in touch. I'll call soon. We need to set up a time for me to come visit."

"Yes. I'd like that." Gabby clicked off the call, thrilled that Jess and Sam were still dating. What were the odds that two shipboard romances were working out?

The next weeks passed in a blur of contentment for Gabby. She continued to make small changes at work, saw Hank most evenings, fulfilled her commitment to Saree and her family, and started to find pleasure in cooking again. But then, Hank was an eager eater who told her how delicious her meals were, inspiring her to create more.

Though they talked of the future, Gabby thought it was too early to move the relationship to the next level, even as she was falling deeper in love with Hank every day.

One evening, Hank called her at the dealership. "Looks like I might be late coming for dinner. Why don't you drive over to Carrington to my business, and we'll take it from there? The French restaurant I like isn't far. We can have a nice luxurious meal there. Sound okay?"

"Yes, I'm always up for a leisurely French meal. What time should I arrive?"

"Why don't we say seven o'clock? After the dealership closes for the night, I'm going to check a few things out. I saw something suspicious on the security footage last night and want to make sure everything is secure."

"Okay, but be careful, Hank. I'll go home and change and then meet you there." Gabby hung up excited for a lovely meal out. She and Hank had been trading meals for a while but being waited on with no cleanup afterward sounded fantastic.

Gabby sat in her office working on the sales figures for the month. Since taking over, sales had improved slightly. She was working on an entire PR media campaign on how buying a new car was a creative way to end winter and begin to enjoy the warmer weather and that buying a new car was like Spring cleaning. She'd created an earlier campaign to draw in more women, and it was working.

She was so embroiled in her work that when she checked her watch, it was almost time to leave for Carrington. Even though it meant she'd be early, she decided to meet Hank without bothering to go home first.

As she entered the town, Gabby was aware of slight differences, making Carrington seem more upscale than Ellenton. The streets were wider with clearly designated bicycle lanes, prettier streetlights lined the roads, and more trees were planted in public spaces.

When she approached the Mercedes dealership, she saw two men in the parking lot. It took her a moment to register that they were fighting. One of the men was Hank, and the other man had a gun.

"Stop!" she shouted, suddenly aware neither man could hear her.

She began beeping her horn.

When the fighting continued, she drove her car up over the curb and onto the grass, shining her headlights on the pair.

She called 911 and opened the car door. "Stop!"

"No, Gabby!" Hank shouted and shoved the man holding the gun.

Gabby heard a loud bang and saw Hank fall to the ground as the man took off running.

Sobbing, Gabby ran to Hank lying on the parking lot pavement. He was bleeding from his left shoulder.

"Oh, my God! Hank! Hank! Are you all right?" She knelt beside him, took off her lightweight jacket, and pressed it up against the wound. Though she was trembling, she tried to remain calm for Hank, telling him over and over again that he was going to be fine.

Hank's eyes remained closed.

"Can you hear me?" Gabby asked. She was shaking so badly that she had a hard time keeping her jacket in place. "I've called 911." The thought of anything happening to Hank brought a sob out of her. "I love you, babe. Stay with us."

Hank's eyes fluttered, and he let out a long groan.

"Don't move," she warned. "I'm here, and help is on the way."

She heard a siren and held back a cry as the sound came closer and closer. She wanted to get up and direct them to Hank, but she knew she had to keep pressure on the wound.

A police car pulled into the lot.

"Here! Over here," Gabby yelled. "We need an ambulance."

Two policemen approached.

"We need medical help," she called to them. "My boyfriend has been shot. Please hurry! He's bleeding badly."

"EMTs are already on their way," said one of the policemen.

Another asked, "What happened?"

"Hank was fighting a man with a gun. The man shot at him and then ran away on foot. I don't know why it would happen." Gabby kept pressure on the wound even as an ambulance pulled up to the scene.

An EMT wearing a blue uniform approached, studying the scene.

"Gunshot to the shoulder," one of the policemen said. "Bleeding badly."

The EMT knelt beside Gabby. "Good thing you've been keeping pressure on the wound. Now, let me see what we're dealing with."

His female partner approached, rolling a collapsible gurney. "Everyone, stand back, please." She knelt beside her partner, wrapped a blood pressure cuff around Hank's uninjured arm, and said quietly, "Let's get him to Ellenton General as quickly as we can."

"I want to go with him," said Gabby standing by, gripping her hands together.

The woman shook her head. "We'll be busy with the patient. Follow us to the hospital. You can meet us there."

"First, we'd better get your car off the sidewalk. How'd it end up there?" said one of the officers.

"I thought if I shone my headlights on them, the attacker would run away," said Gabby, suddenly feeling woozy.

"Why don't I move the car for you. I noticed the keys in it. Do you need us to drive you to the hospital?" a policeman asked.

She shook her head. "Thanks. I'll be all right. Heaven knows how long I'll need to stay there."

The EMTs were rolling the gurney with Hank on it into the ambulance. Gabby ran over to them. "Hank, I love you. Be strong!"

She was unaware of tears rolling down her cheeks until the female EMT handed her a tissue. "We're doing our best to help him. We'll meet you at the hospital."

One of the policemen drove Gabby's car into the lot and parked it. "I've kept the motor running."

Gabby ran over to her car. "Thank you. And thank you for all your help."

She got behind the wheel, took a deep breath, and eased out of the parking spot, reminding herself to drive carefully.

At the ER of Ellenton General Hospital, Gabby announced who she was and why she was there, still feeling as if she was in a nightmare.

The woman behind the reception desk took down the information. "Why don't you have a seat. As soon as the doctors have information to share, they'll let you know."

Gabby walked on unsteady legs to one of the chairs lined up along the wall and sank onto it. She lifted her cell out of her purse and punched in Dan's number.

"Hi, Gabby," he said cheerfully. "What's up?"

A sob caught in her throat.

"Everything all right?" he asked.

"No, it's not," Gabby said and told him about the shooting.

"I'm on my way," Dan said, his voice shaking.

A short time later, Dan walked into the emergency room, saw her, and hurried over. "Any news?"

"Not yet. But I expect to hear something soon."

A nurse entered the emergency room. "Who's here for Hank Davis?"

Both Gabby and Dan stood.

The nurse walked over to them. "I'm supposed to give this to you," she said, addressing Gabby. She handed Gabby a large manila envelope. "It's all of Hank's personal items."

Gabby felt the floor move beneath her at the thought of Hank dying. "Is he..."

"He's going to be fine. He's heading into surgery now. The doctor will explain in a few minutes."

Gabby peered into the opening of the envelope. Hank's wallet, watch, and cell phone were there, along with a small square box. Heart pounding, she lifted the small, black velvet box out of the envelope and stared at it.

"What's that?" asked Dan.

Gabby opened it to find a large, emerald-cut diamond ring.

"Looks like Hank was going to propose tonight," said Dan, putting an arm around her.

Gabby bent over, held her head in her hands, and started sobbing. "Oh, Dan, what if he doesn't survive? There was so much blood."

"Hold on," said Dan, rubbing her back. "You told me earlier he received a shot to the shoulder, and the EMTs arrived quickly. Hank is tough. He's going to get through this. You have to believe it."

They both looked up as a doctor approached them. He gazed around the room and then quietly asked, "Are you here for Hank Davis?"

"Yes, I'm his father," said Dan, helping Gabby to her feet. "How is he?"

"I'm Doctor Todd Mansell. He's about to be wheeled into surgery to take care of some blood vessel issues. The brachial artery, the main artery of the arm, has been damaged. And we want to inspect the brachial plexus, the nerve bundle there. But he's going to be fine. Sore for a bit, I suspect. We'll know more after the surgery."

"Thank you, Doctor. Thank you so much!" Gabby felt her knees become buttery and sank onto her chair.

Dan shook hands with Dr. Mansell. "Thank you for the update. When can we expect to see him?"

"Not for a while," Dr. Mansell said. "The surgery shouldn't take too long, but he'll be in recovery afterward. We'll keep you posted. I suggest you go to the cafeteria and get some refreshments and relax for a bit."

Dan turned to Gabby. "The treat is on me."

"Thanks. I need a cup of tea to steady my nerves." Gabby grabbed her purse, put the ring box she'd been clutching into the envelope holding Hank's belongings, and got to her feet.

"You've been through a lot. Let's sit for a while in the cafeteria. There's something I need to tell you."

Gabby gave him a questioning look, but he remained silent.

Chapter Fifteen

Gabby sat in a booth in the hospital cafeteria opposite Dan sipping on a cup of hot tea, telling herself everything would be all right. But the image of Hank being shot and sprawled in the parking lot hurt and bleeding kept flashing through her mind.

Dan let out a sigh and took a sip of his coffee. "I'm very grateful Hank is going to be all right. I don't know what I'd do if I lost that boy." His eyes filled. "It means so much to me that he decided to come to help me with the business."

Gabby reached across the table and patted his hand. "Hank loves you. He's told me how pleased he is to be here, working with you."

"And now I have something to confess to you. I hope you'll forgive me. You see, there really wasn't a company contest. It was something I made up. Well, your father and I came up with the idea together."

Gabby frowned. "Wait a minute. What do you mean there was no contest? Of course, there was, or I wouldn't have won the tickets."

Dan held up his hand. "Let me explain. There was a contest, but instead of being funded by the company, it was funded by me. However, it was all very proper. You or Hank could've lost the winning tickets by not selling the most cars. That part is true. But I knew the two of you well enough to think that wouldn't happen. You won those tickets honestly."

"So, you paid for the cruise for me?" Gabby asked, confused.

"Yes and no. I paid for the person who fairly won the prize. That was you. However, I encouraged Hank to go on the same cruise to give me a chance to evaluate the other salespeople because I knew a few changes were coming."

"Why would you do that?" said Gabby, giving him a steady look.

Dan's cheeks flushed. "Because your father and I knew if the two of you had a chance to get to know one another away from the business, something might click. You and Hank are a perfect complement to one another. And by going on the cruise with Ashley as she so desperately wanted, Hank could see what a shallow, high-maintenance person she is, how wrong she is for him."

"Heavens! You make Ellie Rizzo seem like a beginner when it comes to matchmaking. And my father went along with it?"

"Your father is the one who thought of it. Having you

settled and happy was his dearest wish before he died. I visited him often while you were at work. We were friends."

Gabby's emotions went from sad, to happy, to shocked. She prided herself on being independent, making her own choices.

"I won them fair and square?"

Dan gave her a troubled look and nodded.

Suddenly, overwhelmed by all that had happened, Gabby burst out laughing. "You two. What a pair!"

Dan held out his hands in a helpless gesture, and then he began to laugh too.

When they finally stopped, Gabby said, "Does Hank know about this?"

"Yes. We talked about it after he told me he was going to propose to you tonight."

"And he was fine with it?"

Dan grinned. "He had the same reaction as you. He laughed, then told me he was glad I'd come up with the plan with your father, that it made it perfect."

"You're right. It does make it seem that way." She smiled at him.

He took hold of her hand. "I've known you since you were a young girl. You're every father-in-law's dream. If you accept Hank's proposal, you'll also make me a very lucky man."

Gabby's vision blurred. She nodded, too grateful to speak.

"Guess we'd better go back and see how our boy is doing, huh?"

Gabby got to her feet. She wanted to see Hank more than anything right now.

⚓

It seemed like days, not a couple of hours, passed before they got the news that Hank was out of recovery.

"He's going to be fine," Dr. Mansell assured them. "We'll keep him overnight to make sure no more bleeding will occur. But then he can go home. We've taken care of what damage he had. We want him to keep that arm stationary for a while. That will necessitate rehab to keep that shoulder moving properly. And with any gunshot victim, we recommend talking to a therapist if needed."

Gabby and Dan exchanged worried looks.

"Can we see him now?" Gabby asked.

"Yes. He's being transported to the surgical section of the third floor. He may be groggy, but he's awake."

"Thank you again, Doctor," said Gabby, accepting a steadying hand from Dan.

They left the waiting area and took the elevator to the third floor, where they were directed to a private room down the hallway.

Gabby wanted to run, but Dan kept hold of her elbow. She'd given Dan the manila envelope, so she and Hank wouldn't be forced to talk about the ring box. That was for another time.

The door to his room was closed.

Taking a deep breath to control her emotions, Gabby opened it and stared at Hank's tall form lying in bed, hooked up to a monitoring device.

"Hey, there," she said softly, approaching him.

He opened his eyes. "Gabby, my angel. I was told you saved my life. Thank you."

"Oh, Hank," she murmured. "You scared me. But Dr. Mansell said you're going to be fine. I'm so glad."

"Hello, son," said Dan, stepping up beside her. "Gave us a scare, but the Davis strength has already come through."

Hank grinned. "Can't keep us down, huh?"

"I'll give you and Gabby some privacy. We'll work out who will pick you up tomorrow morning. I'm so very, very relieved you're okay. I love you, son." He bent and kissed Hank's cheek.

Seeing them together and how much they looked alike, Gabby felt her eyes fill with tears.

Dan put a hand on Gabby's shoulder. "Call me later, okay?"

"Sure. Thanks for everything, Dan. I appreciate it."

He gave them both a quick wave and left the room.

Gabby managed to put her arms around Hank's neck, careful of his shoulder, and kissed him, needing to feel his lips on hers. She'd thought she'd lost him.

"I was so worried about you. What was going on between you and that man, whoever he is?"

"I noticed a photo from the previous night's security pictures that showed a man wandering among the cars on the lot. Something spooked him, and he ran off, but I decided to check around the cars this evening. I saw someone crouching between cars and decided to see what he was up to."

"Did you recognize him?

166

"No, and as I told the police, I'm not sure I could identify him. He was wearing a ski mask both yesterday in the video and today. He also wore black gloves, and there was nothing specific about his clothing. Nothing to help me know who it was. They will continue to handle the case."

She reached up and caressed his cheek. "I'm just so very, very thankful I arrived in time to help. I was going to go home and change my clothes but decided to go there directly from work a little early. It's a lucky thing I did."

Hank smiled sleepily. "Like I said, you're my special angel." He yawned. "We'll talk more tomorrow. Sorry. I can't help it. I'm falling asleep."

"Sleep all you want. That will help you heal." She kissed him again. "Love you."

He squeezed her hand. "Love you, too." He suddenly startled. "Do you have my personal things?"

"Your father does," said Gabby.

"Oh, good. I've got something to ask you." His eyes closed. "Tomorrow."

At home, Gabby felt all her energy leave her as she recalled seeing Hank wounded and bleeding, the drive to the hospital, and then the shocking news Dan told her in the cafeteria. Too exhausted to do more than scramble an egg for dinner, she ate and then headed to bed.

Lying there, she stared up at the ceiling. She'd almost lost Hank. Gabby knew she'd never take spending time with him for granted again. She'd treasure each moment they had together.

She fell into a restless sleep and awoke to a gray, rainy day. Gazing outside, she studied the buds on the trees, the promise of burgeoning green leaves, and thought this second chance with Hank was like the renewal of spring.

She got out of bed and prepared for the day. Dan had called last night and offered to pick up Hank from the hospital this morning. He promised to call her in time for her to meet them at Hank's house. Grateful for his help, she readily agreed, aware Dan wanted alone time with his son.

She ate breakfast, and before she headed into the office, she called Hank.

He sounded cheerful as he said, "Hello."

"Hi. How are you doing this morning? You were still pretty sleepy from the anesthesia when we talked last night."

"I'm sore, but I'm happy to be alive. I understand you saved my life with your jacket. Pretty brave of you."

"You scared me," she said. "I don't know what I'd do if anything happened to you."

"As long as you're with me, I'm not going anywhere if I can help it," he said. "Last night was going to be very special. But don't worry, I'll make it up to you."

Gabby did not indicate that she'd seen the ring. "Just heal well. That's all that's important right now."

"That's not all that's important. But we'll talk later."

"Dan said he'd call when you were approaching your house. I'll meet you there. Can't wait."

"I love you, Gabby. I wouldn't have made it without you."

"Love you too," she said and hung up before she ruined her eye makeup with tears.

When she arrived at her office, several staff members came to see her, asking about Hank. The shooting had made the local nightly newscasts, and they were shocked to know something like that had happened.

"What about security here?" asked a new salesman.

"Dan mentioned he's going to upgrade security at both the dealerships, even though what we have is above standard."

The salesman nodded agreeably, but after he left, Gabby decided to examine the exterior of the building to see for herself. The lot at the Mercedes dealership had been lit, but it was hard to keep space between cars in full light. She knew now she'd been smart to pull the car up onto the grass to shine her headlights on the attacker.

Later, she was working on her spring PR campaign when Dan called. "We're headed to Hank's house now. See you soon."

Excited, Gabby told the receptionist she was leaving.

As she was driving into the front circle of the house, she saw Dan helping Hank out of his car.

They turned and waited for her.

Gabby parked and hurried to them. "Hank, I'm so glad to see you upright and walking."

He held out his good arm, the right one, and she

allowed him to draw her up to him carefully. His other arm was in a sling of sorts, keeping his shoulder secure and his left arm close to his body.

"Glad to see you, too," he said before kissing her.

"Let's get you two inside," said Dan. "I've hired a male nurse to come to help Hank the first few days while he has only the use of one hand and arm. He should be arriving this afternoon."

They entered the house and paused.

"Where would you be most comfortable?" Gabby asked.

"Down here in the den on the couch. I can watch television from there."

"Why don't I get you a warm throw from one of the bedrooms?" Gabby suggested.

"How about the soft blue one in my room?"

Gabby climbed the stairs, pleased to be doing something to help him. When she reached the top of the stairs, she smelled fresh paint and stopped. Puzzled, she glanced around and then went to the master bedroom. The walls had been painted a green lemon color, just the shade of green she would've chosen herself.

She clasped her hands. Hank had told her the room wouldn't be decorated until the right moment. Did this have to do with the engagement ring she'd seen?

She quickly retrieved the blue throw blanket from Hank's bedroom and hurried downstairs.

She spread it over his legs. "There, that should be comfortable."

He pulled her down beside him. "Dad said he'd see us later. Come sit with me."

"I saw the master bedroom," Gabby said.

"Did you like the color? I remembered what you said you wanted."

"Yes, but I was only making a suggestion."

"But it was important to me," said Hank. He sat up. "I know this is a little awkward with me sitting here, but I'm feeling a little off-balance."

He pulled the ring box from his pants pocket. "I'll do this better later, but I couldn't wait to ask. Gabrielle Willetts, I love you and treasure our time together. I've been dreaming of this moment longer than you think. I want to make you happy, be there for you through the good and the bad, just like you've shown me. Will you marry me, my love, my angel?" His eyes filled as he waited for her to speak.

"Yes, oh yes, Hank! I will marry you. I love you, and I always will. The last two days have shown me just how deep that love is."

"Help me open the lid to the box, and then I'll slip the ring on your finger."

Laughing softly, she did as he asked. Staring at the beautiful diamond with fresh emotion, Gabby could hardly believe this gorgeous ring was hers. More meaningful than its beauty was the promise behind it.

Hank brought Gabby to his side. "I adore you. Did Dad tell you the plan he and your father came up with?"

"Yes," said Gabby. "With the two of them working together on us, what chance did we have?"

Hank laughed. "I might have figured it out on my own, but I'm glad they made sure of it."

The cruise was just the beginning of their love story.

Gabby knew that no matter how much time passed, she'd always remember how two fathers had introduced their children to one another. Two smart, loving, kind men.

Gabby snuggled closer to Hank and said a silent prayer of thanks to her father. She and Hank had something special, something more than those winning tickets to treasure.

Dear readers, I hope you've enjoyed having Ellie and John Rizzo (prominent characters in the Sanderling Cove Inn series) on the cruise with Gabby.

Here are the links for the books in that series:

Waves of Hope – https://books2read.com/u/49njyo
Sandy Wishes - books2read.com/u/3G5vjK
Salty Kisses - books2read.com/u/4jgoL2

If you enjoyed sailing with Gabby in The Winning Tickets, leave your troubles ashore and get Lost At Sea with Stevie in Book 8 of the Sail Away Series, a standalone story by author Patricia Sands!
★ **Don't miss a Sail Away book!** ★
(All the books are standalones and can be read in any order.)

Book 1: Welcome Aboard – prologue book

About the Author

Judith Keim, a USA Today Best Selling Author, is a hybrid author who both has a publisher and self-publishes. Ms. Keim writes heart-warming novels about women who face unexpected challenges, meet them with strength, and find love and happiness along the way—stories with heart. Her best-selling books are based, in part, on many of the places she's lived or visited and on the interesting people she's met, creating believable characters and realistic settings her many loyal readers love.

She enjoyed her childhood and young-adult years in Elmira, New York, and now makes her home in Boise, Idaho, with her husband and their two dachshunds, Winston and Wally, and other members of her family.

While growing up, she was drawn to the idea of writing stories from a young age. Books were always present, being read, ready to go back to the library, or about to be discovered. All in her family shared information from the books in general conversation, giving them a wealth of knowledge and vivid imaginations.

Ms. Keim loves to hear from her readers and appreciates their enthusiasm for her stories.

"I hope you've enjoyed this book. If you have, please help other readers discover it by leaving a review on the site of your choice. And please check out my other books and series:

Hartwell Women Series
The Beach House Hotel Series
Fat Fridays Group
The Salty Key Inn Series
The Chandler Hill Inn Series
Seashell Cottage Books
The Desert Sage Inn Series
Soul Sisters at Cedar Mountain Lodge Series
The Sanderling Cove Inn Series
The Lilac Lake Inn Series

ALL THE BOOKS ARE NOW AVAILABLE IN AUDIO. So fun to have these characters come alive!"

Ms. Keim can be reached at www.judithkeim.com

And to like her author page on Facebook and keep up with the news, go to: http://bit.ly/2pZWDgA

To receive notices about new books, follow her on Book Bub:
    https://www.bookbub.com/authors/judith-keim

And here's a link to where you can sign up for her periodic newsletter! https://BookHip.com/RRGJKGN

She is also on Twitter @judithkeim, LinkedIn, and Goodreads. Come say hello!